Indiana Bamboo

Indiana Bamboo

A Novel

Meira Rosenberg

Iris Press
Oak Ridge, Tennessee

Cover Illustration: Jill Sanders
For more information visit www.jsandersdesign.com
or www.jsandersart.com

Author Photo: Dave Rosenblum
For more information visit Images by David
www.imagesbydavid.com

Book Design by Robert B. Cumming, Jr.

Library of Congress Cataloging-in-Publication Data

Names: Rosenberg, Meira, author.
Title: Indiana Bamboo : a novel / Meira Rosenberg.
Description: Oak Ridge, Tennessee : Iris Press, [2017] | Summary: When Paradise Pets, her favorite store in the small town of River Creek, Indiana, is robbed and all the animals vanish, almost eleven-year old Indiana Bamboo and her friends investigate.
Identifiers: LCCN 2017000829 | ISBN 9781604542455 (pbk. : alk. paper)
Subjects: | CYAC: Mystery and detective stories. | Animals—Fiction. | Indiana—Fiction.
Classification: LCC PZ7.1.R672 In 2017 | DDC [Fic]—dc23 LC record available at https://lccn.loc.gov/2017000829

For my extraordinary parents,
whom I miss every day.

For our children and the kiddo,
with so much love.

And always, for David.

ONE

Ding, Da-aa-aa-anggggggggggg.

Someday someone's gonna smash that doorbell, I thought, as I raced to the door.

"Happy Birthday, Indy."

Time out! Stop the presses!

Before I tell you what happened on Sunday, I have to tell you what happened on Thursday, and before I tell you what happened on Thursday, I should properly introduce myself.

My name is Indiana Bamboo.

The true story of how I got my name is that once upon a time, my New-York-City-born-and-bred parents hopped in their car for a little Sunday afternoon drive across the George Washington Bridge. They started talking and talking. And talking. They are real good talkers.

Well, fifteen hours later, when they finally reached an awkward silence in their conversation, they hopped out of the car to get something to eat, except they'd forgotten they weren't in New York City anymore. They were in River Creek, Indiana, surrounded by acres and acres of eight foot high August cornstalks blowing in the wind, and they were mesmerized by the sight of it. Right then and there they decided that girl or boy, they'd name me Indiana, which is just fine with me, because knowing my parents, it could have been a whole lot worse.

They could have named me Cornstalk.

I live in a not quite tumbling-down mansion that, rumor has it, used to be part of the Underground Railroad that my parents rented that very day here in River Creek. Every year my parents try to buy it (the mansion, that is) and every year the realtor says the owner is too busy living off his trust fund, drinking Margaritas, and sailing around the Caribbean to pay attention to business.

I tried sailing once, and I threw up. My best friend Jamie's oldest sister sneaked a Margarita at her parents' Kentucky Derby party last May, and she threw up, so I think the rich guy who owns this house is too busy throwing up all the time to pay attention to business, but the realtor can't say that in polite company.

I don't have any brothers or sisters. I do have four cats, two turtles, a hermit crab, my brand new guinea pig Porky Junior, lots of ladybugs when I can find them, a former boyfriend named Bartholomew Jackson Alexander McGill, and my cousin Boris, who has flaming red hair, lots of freckles like me, and got grounded last week for stealing three packs of gummy worms from the candy store, but Boris is a whole other story.

THIS story begins last Thursday, which happens to have been three days before my eleventh birthday—and the day before the night that Paradise Pets was robbed.

ONE, ALL OVER AGAIN

Last Thursday afternoon, Jamie and I were tooling around on our bikes, me on my good old Red Ranger and Jamie on her new sixteen speed Black Bomber.

We'd cruised halfway across town—which in River Creek takes all of four minutes and twenty-three seconds except for when you get stuck at the red light on Main Street—to get chocolate chip cookies for me and a giant sugar cookie with rainbow sprinkles for Jamie, but I was getting antsy for my daily visit to Paradise Pets. I'd been there every day since two weeks ago Tuesday when the sweetest Cockapoo puppy was delivered.

The cowbell clanged a sour note as we wobbled the wooden door open and walked in.

"Hey, dudes. What's happening?" Hendrix squawked his trademark greeting, flapping his red, blue, and yellow wings for good measure.

Hendrix is a huge, ancient Scarlet Macaw who—cross my heart—is totally psychic. He's lived at Paradise Pets for forty years at least, ever since the owner before the owner before Mr. Humperdink found him parked outside his door one morning with a note taped to his cage that read:

Dudes and Dudettes,
Please take care of me. My owner had to split.
P.S. My friends call me Hendrix.

Jamie patted Hendrix's bright red head while I squeezed through the pet beds piled in the aisles in every size from hamster to Great Dane to find Mr. Humperdink. He was feeding the guppies in the back of the store near Maurice the Bear, Lily, and Esmerelda.

"Maurice!" I smiled and waved. He smiled and waved right back. Then he twirled his purple cape over his arm and tugged his left ear like he always does when he's hungry.

Maurice is a brown bear. He's my other best friend, besides Jamie. Whenever Jamie hollers, "Indiana Bamboo, you have about as much sense as a coconut," and stomps home in consternation, I zip over to Paradise Pets for a cup of lemongrass tea with Maurice. He has to take his tea in his cage. I have to take mine sitting cross-legged with my bony knees just behind the yellow line Mr. Humperdink painted on the floor to keep us kids from getting too close to him. I usually do most of the talking, and Maurice never gets mad, not ever.

Esmerelda is a two-toothed cougar. (Her previous owners weren't big fans of dental hygiene.) Lily is one mangy-lookin' lion whose fur was dyed a mysterious shade of puke mustard yellow before she got here, but you should have seen them when they first arrived. They were just three scrawny, scraggly, sacks of bones.

Maurice has grown downright chubby thanks to Mr. Humperdink's TLC—and more than a few gallons of blueberry-peppermint crunch ice cream from Stefano Stefano's Ice Cream Parlor. I should be happy, but my heart's all tangled up in knots because I know that means he'll be leaving soon.

I waved again to Maurice and blasted my voice over the bubbling fish tanks. "Mis-ter Hum-per-dink!"

Shoulders slumped, Mr. Humperdink shuffled toward me. "What's all the racket?"

"May I please hold Princess Penelope?"

Princess Penelope was lying on her back pumping her pudgy black and white legs in the air, just like the ladies in the Golden Oldies exercise class at Joy-Lynn's Bakery, Exercise Emporium, and Special Occasion Beauty Salon when they do the bicycle with their pudgy legs in the air.

Hendrix zoomed over in a flurry of red, blue, and yellow. "Hold the puppy! Hold the puppy!" he squawked, prying open the latch with his bill and toes.

"No opening the crates!" Mr. Humperdink grumbled, wagging his finger at Hendrix. Then he trudged over to Princess Penelope's cage and plunked the wriggling puppy into my arms. "Indiana, you're going to be one sad girl when someone else takes that Cockapoo home."

"Yes, sir," I said, but I crossed my fingers under Princess Penelope's belly and made a wish no one would.

Jamie sat on an empty crate. She scrunched her eyebrows together in deep thinking mode as a baby guinea pig with a tiny teacup in the middle of its forehead peeked through her cupped hands. "Maybe your Mom and Dad will get her for your birthday, if you promise to walk her and—"

"Nope," I interrupted. "It'll never happen. After I won Bashful at the Shriners' Circus last month, Mom ranted that she was 'up to here in pets and smells' and we were 'DONE! DONE! DONE!' If she lost it over a maintenance-free hermit crab, no way is she letting me have a puppy!"

"When Mr. Porky had her latest litter, Dad stormed around the house muttering, 'I'm shipping them off, every last one!' I wasn't sure if he meant all us girls or all our guinea pigs until he danced around the house singing, 'off to Peru, for guinea pig stew.'"

"Time to go home," called Mr. Humperdink. "Lily needs a stroll out back, and it's time for Maurice's afternoon snack."

"Please let us stay, Mr. Humperdink," I pleaded, trying not to smile so I would look earnest and mature. "Just this once?"

"Absolutely not!" Mr. Humperdink barked as Jamie cringed. "I'd be run out of town faster than you can say Paradise Pets if I had anyone in the store while I'm walking Lily outside in the habitat. It's a near miracle the town of River Creek lets me look after these animals here at all."

I sighed loud enough to make sure Mr. Humperdink heard me. They may be the cuddliest brown bear, mangy-lookin' lion, and two-toothed cougar you'd ever care to meet, but Mr. Humperdink never lets us forget the WILD in those animals. He used to be a world famous Wonderful Wildlife Rescuer before he bought Paradise Pets so he could retire to a nice, quiet life, except the Wonderful Wildlife Rescuers missed him so much they started sending wild animals to him right here in River Creek.

"C'mon girls." Mr. Humperdink frowned.

Jamie snuggled against the guinea pig's tiny cheek.

I hugged Princess Penelope for an extra-long minute.

Mr. Humperdink reached for Princess Penelope with one hand and for the baby guinea pig with the other. "Scram, va-moose, go home!" He shooed us to the door.

But when I turned around to wave good-bye to Maurice, I could have sworn I caught the corner of Mr. Humperdink's mouth curl up, almost in the direction of a smile.

TWO

Two days later they were gone.

Missing. Vanished. Disappeared.

They'd been stolen from Paradise Pets late Friday night.

On Saturday morning, Mom looked deep into my eyes with her "Uh-oh" eyes and handed me the *River Creek Gazette*. The headline alone took up half the front page.

EXTRA EDITION!!!!

PARADISE PETS PURLOINED
Varmints Vanish
Humperdink Hospitalized

River Creek, Early Saturday

Late last night, unidentified thieves broke into the Paradise Pet shop, stealing all the animals, including the bear, lion, and cougar that the owner, formerly famous wildlife rehabilitator Mr. Humperdink, rescued from an illegal carnival last winter.

Suffering from insomnia, Mr. Humperdink reportedly had returned to the store at around midnight. As he walked past the kittens, he felt a terrible pain in the back of his head, only to discover upon waking hours later in River Creek Community Hospital that he had been knocked unconscious with a scratching post.

A teary-eyed Mr. Humperdink told this reporter from his hospital bed, "I haven't been back to the store, but they took all of them, every single one—except Flower." He choked up as his eyes turned to the skunk in her cage near the window.

Mrs. Elsie Conners, the Friday night 911 operator, reported that moments after midnight, a caller speaking in a muffled voice said, "Two guys just robbed Paradise Pets and conked Mr. H."

The police are following every lead and have not ruled out anyone as a suspect. When asked whether the mystery caller was "a good Samaritan or a conscience-ridden accomplice?" Captain Rodriguez, the consummate professional, replied, "No comment."

I sprinted down the back stairs with the rolled up paper in my hand. "Going to Jamie's." I raced past Mom as she tossed me a piece of extra-well-done toast. I hopped on the Red Ranger and pedaled across the street, my brown braids flying behind me. Jamie flew out her front door.

"Did you hear?" she said. "Paradise Pets was—"

"Robbed!" My voice wobbling, I swallowed the lump in my throat, then waved the newspaper. "Did you read—"

"Elizabeth told me," Jamie interrupted.

"C'mon." One of the great things about having a best friend like Jamie is that when it comes to the really important stuff, I never have to explain. She whipped her helmet over her curly black ponytails, hopped on the Black Bomber, and in a flash we were on our way downtown to Paradise Pets.

We parked our bikes and walked slowly toward the store to see for ourselves. When I looked into the windows, reality rose up and punched me clean in the stomach. I tried to catch my breath, but the air drained out of me ---- Pffffttttttttttt ---- fast as a deflating balloon.

No Maurice. No Princess Penelope. No animals at all, not even a guppy. Seeing the emptiness inside felt a thousand times worse than reading about it in the *River Creek Gazette*.

We sat in front of the store in silence.

I glanced at Jamie. Her dark eyes were growing darker as a renegade tear rolled down my cheek. I brushed it away and stood up. "We need ice cream."

We climbed on our bikes and rode. It felt like everyone was moving in slow motion, as if the energy had been sucked out of the whole town. We skidded to a stop at the take-out window of Stefano Stefano's Ice Cream Parlor.

Stefano Stefano's is amazing for two reasons.

The good reason is the blueberry-peppermint crunch ice cream is sublime, and that's coming from me, the world's most devoted chocoholic.

The bad reason is Mr. Stefano Stefano and the nameless Mrs. Stefano have the most terrifying tableside manner any of us kids has ever seen. Jamie and I figure they're drug kingpins, hired assassins, or spies, but so far as I know, every kid who's gone into their ice cream parlor has come out alive, even on Halloween, and believe me, we'd have heard about it if they hadn't.

"I better get going." Jamie licked her sugar cone to catch blueberry drips as I took a bite of my double chocolate Oreo. "I promised Mom I'd help with some errands."

"Let's stop to see Captain Rodriguez on the way home," I said. "Maybe she'll have some news."

We rode down Main Street and swerved into the driveway of the police station, which is actually two rooms in the back of the County Courthouse, and were greeted with a whinny from

Old Blister, River Creek's police horse. His tail was swishing like there was no tomorrow.

"Horse flies bothering you today, buddy?" Jamie shouted.

I pulled the *River Creek Gazette* from my back pocket and swatted. The biting bloodsucker fell to the ground.

Old Blister neighed his approval. He's slow and rickety and deaf as a donut, but once upon a time, he won third place in the Kentucky Derby. It was his one and only moment of glory.

"Indiana, Jamie, let me guess what brings you here on a sunny Saturday," Captain Rodriguez greeted us, peering over the turquoise half-moon reading glasses perched on her nose.

"Did you find them yet?" I burst out, as hyper as the time I guzzled a can of Red Bull and Mom forbade me from drinking it ever again until I'm too old to live at home anymore.

"Not yet. We're working on it." Captain Rodriguez shuffled some papers on her desk.

"Don't you have any suspects?" I asked.

"What about the mystery caller?" asked Jamie at the same time.

Captain Rodriguez held up her hands. "Hold on, girls. How about you give us a little time to solve this thing? It's barely been ten hours since the robbery."

"Ten hours! They could be in Omaha or Tokyo by now."

Jamie winced. Geography isn't exactly what you'd call my strong point, so I may have been off by a mile or two.

"I promise we'll do our best to get every last one of those animals home safely. How about if I get back to tracking them down?"

"Thanks, Captain Rodriguez," Jamie said.

I tried to smile my thanks, but the sadness in my heart cast a shadow that hovered right behind my eyes.

THREE

I rode my bike home, nearly daydreaming my way past the ETCETERA, except the Lylemobile was parked outside, and its particular shade of lime green knocked those daydreams out of my brain. I stopped short because nothing makes a bad day better faster than a visit to the ETCETERA.

Lyle's ETCETERA used to be plain old Lyle's Hardware Store before plain old Lyle got tired of telling Everybody, "I don't just sell hardware, you know." Everybody always answered back, "Yesirree, Lyle, you sell everything but the kitchen sink."

The truth of it was, Lyle would mail order you a kitchen sink if you bugged him enough, but to this day, he refuses to carry high heels, frozen foods, or fresh papayas, but NEVER ask him, "Why papayas?" or he'll go on and on with the saddest love story that will rip your heart clean down the middle and make you wonder why anyone ever bothers with love at all in this world.

I opened the door, and an arctic air blast bounced me halfway out again. Lyle grew up way north in Canada and can't take the, "If the heat don't get ya', the humidity will," Indiana summers.

"Gee-geez, Ly-Lyle," I stuttered, my teeth chattering and eyes watering, "it's cold as a deep freeze in here."

"Why the long face?" Lyle handed me the one-size-fits-all hot pink down parka that he keeps behind the counter for cold customers.

I shrugged on the parka and looked around because there's always something new to see at Lyle's.

Pots and pans, fishing poles, Tonka trucks, and board games hung from the ceiling above the cash register. Beef jerky, Fritos, freeze-dried ice cream, and more candy than I'd ever dreamed could be in one place, from Starburst to Skittles to M&M's and Curly Wurly's, crowded the shelves below.

Best of all, smack in the middle of the store under the twenty foot dome where Lyle had poked a hole in the ceiling, stood a genuine, fifteen foot tall replica of Michelangelo's sculpture of David, flown in direct from Italy. Lyle had gotten so tired of kids skulking around all the time to stare at the "naked guy" that, in honor of his own Scottish roots, he'd dressed David in a giant shirt, kilt, and tam o'shanter.

"They're gone," I finally answered. "Really gone."

"Gone," Lyle echoed. His voice trailed off and his eyes got all dark and faraway.

Lyle was tumbling down deep into one of his spells of lovesickness and heartbreak, and once he tumbled, you might as well have been a can of tomatoes standing there in front of him as a human being.

I had to snap him out of it and quick.

"Oooooooh," I fluttered my eyelids and swooned for dramatic effect. "I think... I think... I'm... dehydrated."

Lyle rushed from behind the register, scooped me up, and lifted me onto a red stool just like the red stools at Stefano Stefano's except without the ice cream. Then he propped my elbows on the counter.

"Holy cow!" He reached into the refrigerator case and pulled out a Snapple. "I almost forgot. This should perk you right up."

"'Peach Mangosteen?'" I read.

"Happy Monday," Lyle said.

Mom only lets me drink one Snapple a week. Lyle and I decided on Mondays so the Sunday night blues don't turn into the Monday morning blahs.

"Thought you'd like to try a new flavor for your birthday tomorrow."

"But today's Saturday."

"True enough," said Lyle, "but with that long face you're wearing, it might as well be Monday."

"Thanks." I sipped in silence for a while. "So," I tore open a pack of Reese's Peanut Butter Cups from the candy shelf, "got any theories about the robbery?"

Lyle leaned in close to me and whispered, "More 'n likely, an inside job."

"You think Mr. Humperdink robbed his own store!"

"NEVER!" He lowered his voice again. "But, you know, if it looks like a rose, and it smells like a rose, it's not a salami sandwich."

Actually, I didn't know. In fact, I had no idea what he was talking about.

"Don't worry," he said. "River Creek's fine police force will crack this case in no time."

I wrinkled my forehead in what Lyle might have interpreted as a not-having-complete-confidence-in-the-River-Creek-Fine-Police-Force face.

"Don't you worry, Indiana," he said. "They're real pros."

"Right." I dug a crumpled dollar bill out of my pocket. "How much do I owe you, Lyle?"

"It's on the house."

"Thanks again, Lyle."

As I walked to the door, I peeled off the crinkly brown paper and popped a Reese's Cup into my mouth. I tried to remember a single big case Captain Rodriguez and Officer Martin had cracked, but I couldn't think of one, unless you counted the Great Lucky's Burger Café non-robbery when I was seven and three quarters.

Captain Rodriguez had busted the case wide open when she discovered that nothing had gone missing, not even a single curly fry, but that Mrs. Lucky Pike had forgotten to lock the front door because she was rushing over to Joy-Lynn's to get her hair done in a French Twist for her daughter's wedding rehearsal dinner in Indianapolis.

I was about to ask Lyle if he could remind me of all the big cases Captain Rodriguez and Officer Martin had cracked, but his eyes looked so dreamy and sad, I knew I'd just turned into that can of tomatoes. So, I put the pink parka on the counter, hung the "Out to Lunch" sign in the window, and pulled the door closed on my way out.

FOUR

The next morning, I woke up bursting with birthday excitement which lasted about a millisecond. Then the loneliest feeling swooped over me as I remembered my nightmare that Maurice was skinny and scrawny again and could barely lift his teacup to drink his lemongrass tea while Princess Penelope was trembling and whimpering in her cage.

It was only five a.m. I was stuck in my room with nothing to do because I'm not allowed to leave my room on weekends any earlier than seven thirty, not even for my birthday, Chanukah, or the Fourth of July.

I was so upset, I couldn't sit still. I hopped and skipped figure eights for six thousand, six hundred and fifty-three hops and skips until I busted out of my room at seven thirty on the dot, raced down the stairs into the living room, and crashed into Mom's plays piled clear up to the ceiling.

By ten o'clock when Jamie was supposed to get here, I'd walked the cats, checked to see if my new birthday cell phone was charged, given my hermit crab Bashful a bath so he'd be nice and clean for my birthday sleepover with Jamie, checked to see if my brand new cell phone was charged, and was perched at the top of the Staircase to Nowhere stacking the last of Mom's plays for her River Creek High drama classes back on top of the pile when—

"Ding, Da-aa-aa-anggggggggggg."

Someday someone's gonna smash that doorbell, I thought, as I flew down the stairs to answer the door.

"Happy Birthday, Indy!"

A gimongous something was sticking out of Jamie's bike basket. It was wrapped in pink, orange, and green tissue paper with blue duct tape stuck every which way and so many holes poked all over they looked like polka dots. Jamie took it out, walked inside, and handed it to me.

"Open it, quick!" Jamie bounced on the balls of her feet. "I hope it cheers you up a little bit."

"Oh my God! It's one of Mr. Porky's babies. It's so cute! Thank you, Jamie. Thank you so much!"

Then, just as fast, I was overcome with sadness. I collapsed into the kitchen chair with my face in my hands.

"Indy, what's wrong?"

"You know I'm not allowed to have any more pets."

Jamie bounced faster on the balls of her feet.

"Why are you so excited?" I asked mournfully.

"I told your mom I'd help you clean the cage twice a week forever if she'd let me give you Porky Junior. She said, 'You've got yourself a deal.' I offered to put it in writing, but she said since she'd known me all my life, a handshake would do just fine."

"Yippee!" I jumped up. "You're the best friend ever."

I threw my arms around Jamie for a three second hug, at least.

I opened the cage and lifted up Porky Junior to look underneath. "What is it? A girl guinea pig or a boy guinea pig?"

"Beats me." Jamie shrugged. "If we were any good at telling the difference, I don't think we'd have named its mama Mr. Porky."

"Okay. She's a girl."

"You can't just declare it, Indiana."

"Sure I can. We just need a proclamation with pomp and circumstance to make it official. Jamie, a drum roll please!"

Da Da Da Dum Da Da Da Dum...

"Baby Porky Junior," I began, as Jamie kept up the drum roll on the kitchen table, "I officially proclaim that you are most officially an official girl, and..."

Buh Dop Buh Dop Buh Dop Buh Dop...

"…henceforth, you shall be known by your official nickname, which officially, and forevermore, shall be... P.J.!

"Follow me!" I ordered Jamie. "We have to introduce P.J. to the cats—even Peek-a-Boo, if we can find her."

"Hold on, Indy. I don't think that's such a good idea. P.J. is so tiny—and tasty-looking. Let's introduce her to Turtledee and Turtledum instead."

"Turtledee and Turtledum aren't cuddly. P.J. needs someone to cuddle up with at night so she's not lonely," I said, as my nightmare about Maurice and Princess Penelope all scared and alone crept back into my brain.

I was halfway up the back stairs when I turned and saw Jamie bouncing on her toes, twirling her curly black ponytails, shaking her head back and forth, and mumbling to herself.

"…eat her... eat her for sure... very sharp teeth... they'll think she's a chipmunk..."

"Jamie, stop mumbling! They're going to love her. She'll be their little mascot."

"Their tasty little mascot," Jamie muttered under her breath.

"It'll be fine. You worry too much." I kissed her cute little nose. P.J.'s that is, not Jamie's.

"Indiana Bamboo," Jamie's voice rose, "you don't worry enough. Should I remind you of the time—"

"No! Geez! You sound like all my worry-disordered worry-wart teachers!"

"The only one with a worry disorder is you. You're missing a major worry gene you, you... worry non-wart!" Jamie shouted.

"Okay, Okay! I'll hold P.J. so tight and you can hold the cats on their leashes. If for some crazy, insane, inexplicable reason they don't adore P.J., we'll protect her."

"You promise not to let go of her, no matter what?"

"Yes!"

"All right, I'll come. But only because you need me to protect P.J.," Jamie agreed.

We tiptoed up to three of our four cuddly cats who were sleeping in front of the old radiator in my parents' bedroom. While Jamie looked under the dresser for Peek-a-Boo, I clicked leashes on their collars. They all must have had some night last night because they were out cold.

"Miss Softie, Explorer, and Stray Frederick Greasepaint, I'd like to introduce you to Porky Junior. P.J. for short."

The cats didn't budge, but P.J. twitched her whiskers up and down fast as a tiny propeller. She couldn't wait to meet them. I squished next to Miss Softie so P.J. could sniff her, whiskers to whiskers, when all of a sudden, Miss Softie opened one eye, hunched up her back, and let out the loudest yowling hiss in tarnation.

Jamie yelped. P.J. wriggled out of my hands and scurried across the floor under my parents' king-size bed. Miss Softie charged under the bed after P.J. while a black shadow—Peek-a-Boo—scooted out of the room.

"Jamie, the leash! Step on Miss Softie's leash!"

"I've got it!" Jamie cried.

I dove down and scooched back and forth to get as far under the bed as I could.

"I don't see her. P.J.'s not here."

"She ate her! Miss Softie swallowed her whole. P.J. is gone." Jamie choked out her words as tears filled her eyes. "I knew this was a stupid idea. I knew it. I knew it. I knew it."

"Jamie!" I slid out from under the bed. "Miss Softie is a cat, not a snake. She can't swallow P.J. whole."

"You don't know that, Indiana. Cats are ruthless predators. My birthday gift to you could be waiting helplessly in Miss Softie's stomach right now, hoping against hope that somehow, someone will save her."

I rolled my eyes, but when Jamie wasn't looking, I squooshed Miss Softie's belly to check for unusual bulges. Then I locked the cats in the kitchen so we could search the entire upstairs.

We searched every inch of my parents' bedroom, every inch of my bedroom, and every inch of the sunroom. We searched my dad's study, my mom's study, the sewing room, my playroom, and all three upstairs bathrooms.

We couldn't find P.J. anywhere.

A picture popped into my head and a smell socked me in the nose from the winter when I was five and a squirrel got trapped in the wall of our house. We didn't know it until the poor critter died of starvation. We had to have someone come to open the wall because the stench was so bad it flipped my stomach sideways, inside out, and upside down.

Now poor baby P.J. was trapped forever in the wall of death. If I had better worry-genes, this never would have happened.

FIVE

"It's all my fault," I moaned. I stretched out across my parents' bed, placed my forearm across my forehead in desperate damsel mode, and closed my eyes.

Jamie plunked down next to me.

"I think I only have a single, solitary worry-gene which is so busy worrying about Maurice and Princess Penelope, that it can't worry about anything else, and now poor P.J. is trapped and starving in the wall of death."

"She isn't starving in the wall of death. She hasn't even been lost for an hour! If one of your feline predators didn't chew her to bits, P.J. could be hiding anywhere in this tumbling-down mansion of yours."

"Holy Guacamole. You're right." I jumped up and tugged Jamie's sleeve. "C'mon, stop moping around. We're not giving up now!"

"Here P.J.! Come out, come out wherever you are," I called, as we walked up the stairs to the third floor. Jamie grabbed the emergency flashlight from an electric outlet and raced ahead while I dropped down on my hands and knees to search the hallway. My bony knees crunched with pain on the wooden floor, but I crept back and forth like a lawnmower so I wouldn't miss an inch.

"Here P.J., P.J., P.J." I crawled to the back of the hall, up to the tiny alcove behind the stairs to the roof when—

Oh... My... God! My heart thumped. Loud thumps. I couldn't think or breathe.

Black basketball sneakers nearly hit me in the face. Beatup, broken-down black basketball sneakers. I froze. *I don't own black basketball sneakers*, a voice in my head shouted while at the same time I saw ankles. Hairy ankles. Hairy ankles attached to the feet wearing the black basketball sneakers.

I forced my eyes to unfreeze and rotated my eyeballs just enough to see that those hairy ankles belonged to a sleeping boy with a dirty face, stringy blond hair, and a squashed stovepipe hat.

"Aaaaaaahhhhhh!" I screamed.

"Aaaaaaaahhhhhhh!" the boy screamed, jolting upright.

"Aaaaaaaaahhhhhhhh!" Jamie screamed, racing from the yellow guest room into the hallway.

"AAAAAAAAAAAHHHHHHHHHHHHH!" Jamie and I screamed in each other's faces. My brain commanded, "Run feet. Run," but my feet no longer understood English.

We both turned to the boy. He was gone.

"Where is he?" Jamie looked around.

I raced up the rickety staircase to the roof, though he'd have to have run faster than a Thomson's gazelle to have escaped without our noticing. The door to the roof was still locked from the inside, but there was no place else he could have gone.

Jamie and I had spent our whole, entire lives knocking on walls and looking under staircases—all six of 'em counting the Staircase to Nowhere—in our never-ending search for the secret passageways that the runaway slaves used while escaping to freedom on the Underground Railroad.

We'd found nothing. Nada. Zip.

"This is it, Jamie." My heart was pounding with excitement. "This is the moment we've been waiting for." I paused for dramatic effect. "We've finally seen a ghost."

"There's no such thing as ghosts." Jamie raised her left eyebrow, looking unimpressed. "He must have been a hallucination."

"What did your hallucination look like?" I asked.

"He was a boy sleeping on the floor, sticking halfway out of the alcove under the stairs, with black sneakers, a dirty face, very untidy clothes, and a stovepipe hat pulled kind of low on his forehead."

"Like President Lincoln's hat, but dirty and crushed?"

"Exactly!"

"That was my hallucination." I folded my arms across my chest.

"Wow!" said Jamie.

"Not 'Wow!' People don't have the same hallucination because hallucinations come from deep inside your own brain. He was a ghost."

"He was not a ghost. If you're so sure he's not a hallucination, that leaves only one other choice. He's a real boy." Jamie pressed her lips tight.

"For cryin' out loud, he isn't Pinocchio. He's a ghost and we're going to find him," I argued. "He has to be here somewhere."

Except that in all my imaginings, ghosts were at least a little bit transparent. This ghost was solid and smelly, and worst of all, as far as my ghost imaginings went, were those hairy ankles. I was having doubts about my first encounter with the other side, but I wasn't admitting a thing.

I squeezed inside the tiny alcove, but it was too dark to see, so I ran my palms along the wall. At first, there was nothing very interesting, just the same old scratchy bumps in the paint that had always been there every other time we'd searched for secret passageways.

Then I felt something. Toward the middle of the wall. A long, skinny crack that I'd never felt before.

"Jamie, quick, shine the flashlight where my hands are!"

Jamie crouched into the alcove. "It's a little door."

I gently tapped the door until I could edge my thumb under the corner and pry it open.

"Whoa! Where did that come from?" Jamie reached for the wall.

"Be careful—don't push it closed."

We both leaned over to stare inside.

The little door opened to a chute that went straight down—down past the narrow stream of light from the flashlight, down further and further until there was just darkness.

"It must have been sealed shut." I poked my head further in and felt around. The chute was about two feet wide, and the sides were dusty, but smooth. "I'm going down."

"Are you nuts?" said Jamie. "This could go straight into the furnace."

"No way. It's probably an old laundry chute or something." I climbed in and began to slide before Jamie had a chance to stop me.

She shined the flashlight down the chute. "Everything okay, Indy?"

"Meet me in the basement."

"Basement... basement... basement...," my voice echoed as I slid faster and faster. The flashlight beam grew dimmer and dimmer, then disappeared altogether. A whoosh of panic poured through my body, landing right in my churning stomach. It was pitch black.

The chute closed in on me. I could hardly breathe. I was going to drop off into nothingness and be stuck forever in this wall of death like the squirrel and poor P.J., whom I'd almost forgotten.

"Owww!" I landed smack hard on a pile of coal.

As I stood up and began to dust myself off, a hand reached around and covered my mouth.

And my heart fell into my still churning stomach.

Six

"...ET... UR... AND... OFF... EEE!" I shouted as loud as I could considering that there was a hand pressing against my mouth.

"Shhhhhh! Zip it. Someone's gonna hear you," the ghost said in a low voice.

Except he looked like a real boy, and he sounded like a real boy, but it was the smell that clinched it. He smelled too gross to be a ghost. I was practically suffocating from the yucky dirt smell of his hand contaminating my nostrils.

"...OOVE... UR... AND." My muffled shouts vibrated inside my head like I was underwater.

"I'm gonna take my hand away, but if you scream again, it's goin' right back."

It was then I noticed that I was a good head taller than this filthy intruder. I pushed his hand off, bent his left arm behind his back, and held him prisoner.

"Oww! What'd you do that for?"

"What did I do that for? WHAT DID I DO THAT FOR? You assault me in my own home in which you are an intruder, I risk my life sliding down a dusty, dark, secret laundry chute and just about kill myself on an ancient pile of coal so I can catch you, and you ask me that stupid question. Jamie, call the police.

"Jamie?"

Jamie didn't answer. I thought she might not have made it downstairs yet, so I turned around to see. There she was, standing with one hand on her hip and her chin in her other hand while she gave the boy the once over. Considering Jamie's worrisome nature and general nervousness, she looked uncharacteristically calm.

"Show me your eyes," she ordered, bending down a little and tilting her head so she could get a better view of his eyes hidden under the brim of his hat.

"What for?" He sounded about as puzzled by her demand as I was.

"You live on North Sixteenth Street?"

"Who wants to know?" he grumbled.

"Oh for Pete's sake," I said, though I thought Jamie had lost her mind. "There are only three of us in here. Who do you think wants to know?"

"I'll tell you if you promise not to call the police," he answered.

"No way! You must be out of—"

"Depends," Jamie interrupted. "Why'd you break in here?"

"I ran away. The kitchen door was open, and I saw the back stairs, so I just kept going up."

"Jamie," I waved my free arm, "what are you doing? He could be a murderer!"

"He's no murderer, Indiana. He's a Weaver."

The boy turned pale under all that dirt. "Oh yeah? Prove it."

"For starters," Jamie raised both eyebrows, and I swear, she pointed them straight at him, "you have smoky gray eyes."

It was my turn to scrunch down and stare with my hand on my hip. I crinkled up my hazel green eyes to take a good look. He had smoky gray eyes, all right. All five Weaver boys and their dad are famous in River Creek for those smoky gray eyes.

The Weavers are famous in River Creek for another reason, too. Last summer, Mrs. Weaver flew the coop. She went to Italy for an astrology or anthropology—or maybe it was cosmetology—week-long conference, and didn't come back until the day before Thanksgiving. Now Mrs. Weaver is living in their house, and Mr. Weaver is living eight miles down the road in a room at the Libertyville YMCA.

"You're Tom, right? You were in Mr. Bryant's fifth grade class when we were in fourth grade," said Jamie. "We've seen you helping Horrible Humperdink at the pet store, and I met you once a couple of years ago when my sister Elizabeth snuck out to meet your brother Cody. They dragged us along and made us go to some stupid baby movie just so they could make out the whole time."

"Yeah—your sister's nice. She dated Cody for a real long time. I think they just got back together."

"Back together…?" Jamie was too stunned to say another word.

When Jamie's parents found out that Cody had almost been sent to Juvie for stealing from Angel's Video Games, they'd put the kibosh on that romance in a New York minute. This was a new side of Elizabeth, a sneaky, love-struck side of the most perfect of Jamie's four perfect, popular, everything-ly gifted, and to top it off, not the least bit conceited, older sisters.

They broke the mold before Jamie came along—well, not exactly the mold since all five Doolittle girls are adopted from different countries, except Jamie says her claim to fame is she's a Heinz 57, one-of-a-kind, American kid—but I think Jamie's the most interestingly gifted of all. It's just that her giftedness is more subtle.

"Hey, don't change the subject." I narrowed my eyes at Tom and tried to act tough while I tightened my grip on his arm. "If you're not a murderer, then what are you doing sleeping in my house, Tom Weaver?"

It was his turn to act tough. "I'll tell you if you want me to." He lowered his voice to a husky whisper. "But you might not want me to. And you can't tell anyone where I am."

"Start talking," I commanded. "We'll stop you if we don't want to hear any more."

"You have to let go of my arm first."

We stared each other down. I was sure he wanted to bolt, but I let go. I figured I could grab him again if I had to.

"You can't tell. You have to swear."

"We won't," Jamie promised, raising her palm. "I swear."

Tom crossed his arms and waited.

"Fine. I swear, too," I said. "But you better not be a murderer or I'm goin' back on my oath."

"It's kind of a long story," he began.

I leaned against the wall to listen. Jamie sat on an overturned bucket.

"I guess you heard about Paradise Pets? Mr. Humperdink's store?"

"What of it?" I asked, wavering between toughness and tears.

"Well, that's it. That's why I'm hiding."

SEVEN

Jamie and I looked at each other. My eyes popped halfway out of my head. Jamie's brown eyes were round as plums.

"You robbed Horrible Humperdink's store?" Jamie jumped up.

"Why would you do a dumb thing like that?" I balled my hands into fists, ready to conk him before he had a chance to do any head conking around here.

Tom scowled. "I never said I robbed him."

"The newspaper said the store was robbed sometime around midnight. What were you doing there if you didn't do it?" I asked, in the meanest TV police detective-type voice I could muster.

"I was asleep in the storeroom."

"Why?" I blurted too loud while Jamie raised her right eyebrow and waited for Tom to say more.

"I dunno." Tom shrugged. "Sometimes I just like sleeping there, near the animals."

I jabbed the air with my index finger. "You expect us to believe that you'd rather sleep on the cold, hard floor of a crowded storeroom than in your own warm, soft bed?"

Tom shrugged again and blushed bright fuchsia from the dirty creases in his neck clear up to his stringy blond bangs.

Jamie aimed her right eyebrow at me to shut me up—she is truly gifted with those eyebrows of hers—then looking directly at Tom, as if he looked perfectly normal with a fuchsia face, she asked, "If you didn't rob Horrible Humperdink's store, why are you hiding?"

"If you want me to tell you any more, you're gonna have to stop calling him that," Tom frowned.

I tried to hide the surprise busting out all over my face at the discovery that I wasn't the only kid in town who didn't call him Horrible Humperdink.

"Okay, okay," Jamie muttered, "but I still think he's an old grump."

"So—why are you hiding?" I asked.

"Because I saw the two guys who robbed the store, and one of them saw me right back. He threw a real strange look in my direction, like he recognized me or something."

"It's those eyes, Weaver. It's those smoky gray Weaver eyes," I said, without thinking about how it sounded until the words had already tumbled out of my mouth. I had to take deep breaths and think about evil, disgusting Brussels sprouts to keep from going fuchsia-faced because I knew it sounded like I liked his eyes, which I did, but not in the way I thought he might think I did.

"What did the thieves look like?" Jamie asked while I was still deep breathing.

"Big." Tom stood on his toes and stretched his arms out as far as they'd go to describe them. "Really big. One guy had buzzed brown hair, and the other guy had messy red hair, but they had smudged charcoal or something on their faces and wore bandanas across their mouths, so I couldn't tell much."

For a split second, a picture of my cousin Boris and his messy red hair flickered across the movie screen in my brain. I wouldn't put it past him to steal a puppy or two, but an entire pet store is definitely out of his larcenous league—besides the fact that he's only twelve years old, short, skinny, and millions of miles away.

"And there was something weird about the whole thing," Tom continued.

"Of course it was weird," I agreed. "I mean guppies! Who steals guppies?"

"Yeah." Tom nodded. "I hadn't thought of that. But what I meant was that it was too quiet. I didn't hear a single bark. No meows, no squeals, no nothin'. Not even any grunts or growls from Maurice, Lily, or Esmeralda."

"How'd they get a chubby brown bear, a mangy-lookin' lion, and a two-toothed cougar to walk out without a sound?" Jamie asked.

"I dunno, but the weirdest part was that Hendrix didn't make a single squeak or squawk," and as Tom's smoky gray eyes grew even smokier, I got the feeling he cared a lot about that bird.

"That doesn't make sense at all. If there were a reality TV show called *American Chatterbox,* Hendrix would win in a heartbeat," said Jamie.

"So, were you in the storeroom when you saw them?" I asked.

"Yeah. I was dozing on and off when all of a sudden I heard someone yell. I jumped up and looked from the doorway of the storeroom into the store. Mr. H. must have walked in on them and gotten conked right then because I saw him fall into a heap on the floor."

"Whoa," Jamie murmured.

"Holy Guacamole." I stared at Tom. "Did you see them conk him?"

"Nah. Brown-buzz guy was already halfway out the back door with a bunch of sleeping puppies in his arms, but Messy-red-headed guy spotted me, did a double-take, and stopped short."

"Why didn't he conk you?" I asked.

"He wanted to. I ducked as he started toward me. He said something that I couldn't hear to Brown-buzz guy, who answered him pretty loud, 'You're seein' things, you idiot. I told you to lay off the hooch tonight!'"

"Whoa," Jamie murmured again. "You must have been petrified."

"Yeah, but I was more scared for Mr. H. He was out cold, and he had a big bump on the back of his head. I called 911, then—"

"*You're* the mystery caller!" My mouth dropped to my toes in astonishment.

Jamie wagged her arms impatiently. "Go on, go on!"

"I saw a black panel truck parked outside before they left, so I ran out and looked up and down the street to see which way it went, but it was a real foggy night and it disappeared. I stayed with Mr. H. until I heard the ambulance sirens. It wasn't until I was just about to go that I noticed Flower shaking in her cage with her rear end up trying to spray."

"They left Flower?" asked Jamie.

"Yeah. I guess they were scared she'd spray 'em," Tom said.

"You know what that means, don't you? They can't be from around here if they don't know about Flower." Jamie began bouncing on her toes.

"No way," I agreed. Whenever the *River Creek Gazette* can't find anything exciting happening in town, they write about how Mr. Humperdink found Flower trapped in the garbage bin behind his store, and how she looked so sad and pitiful he had her scent glands removed so he could keep her.

"How come Horr... Mr. Humperdink came back to his store at midnight anyway?" Jamie asked.

"Ever since Mrs. H. died last year, he's been spending more and more time at the store after closing up. I come over late sometimes to sort of check up on him." Tom raised his shoulder in an embarrassed half-shrug. "He just sits there with Flower in his lap for hours and hours, with a real sad look on his face."

"He was always so grouchy, I thought it was his natural temperament. I never thought of him as having a wife—or losing one. You just don't know about people." Jamie shook her head in wonderment.

After a minute I asked, "Why'd you leave before the paramedics got there?"

It didn't make sense. I was beginning to wonder if Tom was trying to pull something over on us after all.

"Yeah," Jamie added. "You're, like, the key witness. You should go to the police."

Tom reached up and began twisting his left earlobe. I thought he was going to twist it off by the time he answered.

"I can't."

"Why not?" Jamie asked. "You saw the bad guys."

"I mostly only saw their hair. Except..."

"What?"

Tom closed his eyes. "Messy-red-headed guy's bandana sort of slipped on his way out, and I sort of got a glimpse, but I don't know if he glimpsed me glimpsing him. It wasn't even much of a glimpse."

"Jamie's right. You have got to tell the police," I insisted.

"If I tell, those guys will know it's me. If they don't kill me, my parents will when they find out I slept at Paradise Pets. Besides, the police would never believe me."

"That's ridiculous," said Jamie. "Of course they'll believe you."

"No way. They'll think I'm lying or trying to get attention, or worse, that I had something to do with hurting Mr. H."

"Why would they think that?" Jamie asked.

"Mr. Humperdink can tell them how much you help out at the store and—" I began.

"Forget it." Tom paced back and forth. "I guess you and everybody else in town know that Officer Martin arrested my brother Cody for shoplifting a couple of video games a few months ago."

Jamie and I half-nodded, not sure whether to admit that everybody did know, since everybody knows everything about practically everyone around here—even when you've never ever met the everyone you know everything about.

"After that, Officer Martin was on us like glop on glue. He said now that we're from a 'broken home,' it was his duty to make sure we don't slide down 'the slippery slope to the deep pit of criminality.'"

"Just because your parents are separated? That's so lame!" Jamie exclaimed.

"Cody never meant to steal those video games. He ran out of Angel's with the games in his hand when he saw Elizabeth walk by. Just his luck, Officer Martin happened to be riding past on Old Blister."

"One teenager accidentally shoplifts in River Creek, and Officer Martin thinks it's the start of an uncontrolled crime spree," I remarked.

"Love sure seems like a lot more trouble than it's worth," Jamie said.

From my experience with Bartholomew Jackson, I couldn't have agreed more.

"You think those guys are coming back for you?" I stared at Tom.

"Yeah." He twisted his poor earlobe even harder than before. "Maybe."

Jamie's eyes rounded into plums again. "What are you going to do?"

"Keep hiding, I guess."

"You can't hide forever," Jamie said.

"Yeah—you can't exactly go into the Federal Witness Protection Program," I added. "You're just a kid."

"You got any better ideas?" Tom asked.

"Not yet."

Then I sat stick straight on the coal room floor, closed my eyes, pressed my hands against my head real hard with my elbows pointing straight out, and waited for a wondrous idea to pop into my brain.

EIGHT

I waited.

And waited.

Jamie and Tom stared. And stared some more.

Jamie figured I'd come up with something good any second. Tom probably thought I'd gone bonkers, but my mind was blank. Completely. Which was not a condition I was used to.

My brain was usually so chock full of ideas, they crashed around like bumper cars at the Indiana State Fair. Not this time. This time my brain was chock full—of silence. Silence swooshed between my ears. Silence boomed behind my eyeballs. Silence sucked up every molecule of oxygen in the small room until it felt like I was breathing pure coal dust.

A line of perspiration dripped down from my forehead, tickled my temple, then trickled down my cheek. I needed to get some air.

And that's what did it. I must have stirred up a bunch of neurons when I stood up because a spotlight turned on inside my head and the word "CLUES" tap-danced across the movie screen in my brain.

"Clues," I said. "We have clues!"

"What clues?" asked Jamie.

"Follow me," I said, as if it had something to do with my big revelation. The truth is, I was starting to feel panicky in a claustrophobic sort of way. My eyes watered, and I could hardly breathe. Jamie and Tom seemed oblivious to the fact that we were edging closer to black lung disease by the second.

Covered with soot from head to toe, I tiptoed up the creaky basement stairs into the kitchen. Jamie and Tom followed on my heels.

"Wash up, you guys, so we don't get fingerprints all over the walls. That's the one and only thing that drives my dad bananas," I said, scrubbing my hands and trying to blow the soot out of my nose.

"So, Indy, how're we going to get clues?" Jamie nudged me over to wash her hands.

"We have a bunch already." I dried my hands on a towel that was turning blacker and blacker. "C'mon, we'll think better in Fort Bamboo."

"Fort...?" Tom began.

Jamie pushed past him. "Just the best tree house in the galaxy!"

"Last one there's a rotten egg." I raced out the back door.

I tapped a knot in the tree with the secret code—

Long, long, long   short, long, long, short   short   long, short

—and the automatic rope ladder unrolled and swung down. I grabbed it and climbed up with Tom following behind me. Jamie, who's the fastest tree climber in River Creek, and more 'n likely the world, shimmied up the oak and got there before we did.

"Wow," Tom said, weaving through rows and rows of origami cranes in every imaginable color—from purple, pink, turquoise, and red to chartreuse with pumpkin polka dots—hanging from the ceiling, on the walls, and on the branches drooping above us.

"Jamie made the cranes, all gazillion and one of 'em. She's the genius queen of origami." I smiled.

Jamie scrambled up to the top bunk of the quadruple bunk beds while Tom settled into the cornstalk recliner.

"Grape Guts, Lemon Splash, or Tangerine Tango?" I pointed to the small soda fountain sliding out from inside the tree. "Unless you'd like another flavor?"

"Naturally sweet. Sugar free," Jamie explained. "Indy's mom ix-nayed the ugar-shay 'cause we drink a lot of this stuff. It makes any flavor we say out loud."

"Dad's working on a way for it to sense the flavors we're in the mood for without saying them, but no luck so far. Every time I think of strawberry, I get spinach-pickle punch." I shuddered, then folded three origami cups and filled them up. When it comes to origami, cups are where my talent begins and ends.

"Hey—how did you do that?" Tom asked, watching Jamie's hand wipe disappear.

"Indy's dad invented a way to stabilize hand sanitizer into a paper-like texture for when you want something more substantial than liquid. Cuts down on wasted paper towels, too."

"Your dad's invented cool stuff," said Tom.

"That's nothing. You should see our garage."

Jamie gulped down her Lemon Splash and held her cup under the fountain for another. "Now what?"

"Time to figure out our clues." I refilled Tom's Grape Guts and climbed up on my Toad Stool. "Are you sure you didn't sleep through all the noise when the robbers stole the animals?"

"I'm positive. I always wake up when the animals do."

"Very fishy, don't you think?" I said, tapping my temple. "How could those robbers get all the puppies and kittens, not to mention a bear, a lion, and a two-toothed cougar, out of there without just one little roar?"

"How about Hendrix? He should have been squawking up a storm," Tom added.

"Maybe they knocked you out. Did you have a headache or anything when you woke up?" Jamie asked.

Tom shook his head.

"Maybe they drugged you," I suggested.

"That's it!" Tom whooped with excitement.

"You were drugged!"

"I knew it!" Jamie and I exclaimed at the same time.

"Not me. The animals," said Tom.

"How do you drug a cat?" Jamie asked.

Tom thought for a minute. "You could give it a shot like people get before an operation."

"Or a rag dipped in ether held over its nose like in Sherlock Holmes movies," I added.

"How about Benadryl? It always makes me sleepy," said Jamie.

"The animals must have been drugged somehow. That's clue number one. We just have to find out how. Number two clue is that we figured the robbers weren't from around here because they didn't know Flower couldn't spray 'em, but Messy-red-headed guy recognized Tom—that's clue number three—"

"Which makes no sense at all if they're not from around here," said Jamie.

Tom frowned. "But it has to mean something. I don't know how or why, but that guy knew me. I'm sure of it."

"And we know Tom didn't do it. That's clue number four." Jamie smiled shyly at Tom.

"Yeah." I gave Tom my most piercing look. "I guess if you'd done it, you wouldn't be hiding out from the guys who did, and you'd have a truckload of animals or money to show for it."

"Shouldn't you call your parents?" Jamie asked. "They must be worried sick. My mom starts calling out the National Guard if we're even fifteen minutes late."

"Haven't your parents been calling you on your cell phone?" I asked.

"No and no. I don't have a cell phone, but if I did, my parents wouldn't know they should be worried yet because of being separated."

"What does being separated have to do with anything? They must still be worried."

I'd done it again. Jamie gave me the evil eyebrow as the fuchsia blush crept up and up from the dirty lines on Tom's neck.

"My parents don't speak." Tom crinkled the damp origami cup in his hand.

"You mean like a vow of silence? That is so cool. I've always thought I'd be really good at a vow of silence like those monks who—"

"No, Indiana," Tom interrupted. "They speak. Just not to each other."

"Oh," I said, and I did not so much as glance at Jamie because I did not want to see what my foot in my mouth was making her eyebrows do now.

"So, I kind of have a system. I can't take credit for it 'cause my older brothers invented it. Whenever I need to, I tell Mom I'm at Dad's, and I tell Dad I'm home with Mom. They're pretty new at this being separated thing, so they're not onto us yet."

"Don't they call you to say good night?" I asked.

"My mom checks on us all the time when she's not home," Jamie said, "but she always asks my older sisters the same thing. 'Did you feed the guinea piggies?' She never asks them if they've fed me. You've got to wonder where I stand on the totem pole of her love."

I rolled my eyes. Jamie can see her parents practically all day long because they're pediatricians, and their office is in a converted barn in their backyard. Plus, Jamie's freezer is jam-packed with everything from chicken pot pie and chocolate chip waffles to blueberry-peppermint crunch ice cream.

Unlike my freezer. One of these days, my parents are going to win the *Guinness World Record* for "Most Absentminded Adults on Planet Earth." They'd starve to death if I wasn't around to remind them to buy groceries.

"So what are you going to do?" Jamie asked as I was thinking about warm, crunchy, chocolate chip waffles.

Tom looked down at his black sneakers. He took a deep breath. Then he looked right at me.

"I was hoping that I could stay here."

NINE

"Here?" I stared at Tom.

"I mean, it doesn't have to be in Fort Bamboo." He blinked. "I could just hide out in your attic for a while until Messy-red-headed guy and Brown-buzz guy get caught."

"Don't you have to go home? How many days have you been away?" Jamie asked.

"You can't go home. If Messy-red-headed guy knows who you are, he might know where you live," I said.

"Yeah." Tom twisted his left earlobe again. "But I have to check in soon—somehow. I've been gone for three nights already. I think I've got until lunchtime before Mom figures out that I'm missing and calls in the troops."

"What if the robbers are spying on your house?" Jamie asked.

"You'll have to go home under cover of darkness!" I swished my arm through the air.

Jamie raised her left eyebrow in a "speak English" sort of way. "Darkness? At lunchtime?"

I tried to raise my eyebrow back at her, then stopped when I saw Tom staring at me. "You know your way around your house a lot better than the robbers do. We'll spy on your house to spy on the robbers to see if they're spying on you."

Tom nodded. "I can do it if you'll be my lookouts. I'll sneak in the hidden den window in the back. It's blocked by shrubs so no one will see me. Cody taught me how to jimmy it open so I wouldn't tell on him for sneaking in late one night."

"Cody? Was he with... never mind." Jamie shook her head. "What if the robbers never get caught? They'll get you if you stay home, but you can't hide out and sneak around forever."

"Thanks, Jamie." Tom grimaced. "You're a real optimist."

"Well, we're just going to have to solve this petnapping fast. C'mon you guys." I hopped off my toad stool.

Jamie jumped down from the bunk. "Where are we going?"

"To the scene of the crime," I replied. "Where else?"

"We'd better change into clean clothes. We won't get past our parents or anyone else looking like this. Meet you on terra firma." Jamie wrapped her arms around the tree trunk and shimmied down.

I pulled over the rope ladder and zipped down the rungs. Tom zipped down behind me.

"I can't go back to the pet store. I'll either get arrested by the police or pounded by the petnappers."

"But you're the only witness! You're the only one who knows that the animals were completely, totally, weirdly silent," I said, as we walked inside and ran up the back steps two at a time. "Mr. Humperdink couldn't know 'cause he was conked out."

"You can do it without me," Tom said.

"You have to go back." Jamie insisted. "You might notice something no one else would see."

I turned to face Tom as we stopped on the second floor landing. "Why are you so worried about getting arrested anyhow? The police don't know you were there."

"You saw what it said in the paper, didn't you?" Tom's voice rose. "That the police have leads about the mystery caller's identity."

"They say that all the time so the public doesn't freak out," I said. "Imagine how it would sound when a dangerous criminal is on the loose if they announced, 'Sorry folks. No leads. We have nothing. Zilch. Zippo. And by the way, sleep tight and sweet dreams.'"

"Nope." Tom shook his head. "Not going. Too risky."

"You're right," I proclaimed, a little louder than I meant to. "Maybe it's too risky for a boy named Tom Weaver to go back to the store. But a girl named Tammy can."

"Who?"

"You! No one will recognize you dressed like a girl."

"It's perfect!" Jamie exclaimed. "That way you can come with us, and then you can go home without being spotted if the bad guys come back."

"You two are nuts! I'm not dressing up like a girl."

"You have to! There's no other way. You can shower up on the third floor while Jamie and I get cleaned up in my bathroom."

I rummaged through my drawers, digging out t-shirts, shorts, and skirts, then tore through my closet until I found the perfect outfit. I raced up the stairs, knocked on the bathroom door, and called to Tom that I was leaving his clothes outside.

Halfway down the stairs, I heard a yelp.

"No way!" Tom hollered, slamming the bathroom door shut so hard the stairs quaked. "Forget it!"

When I went back upstairs after my shower, Tom was not a happy camper. His face was clean, but he was wearing his same old clothes and his dirty old hat.

"You expect me to wear these?" He held up a lavender, long-sleeved blouse, a jean skirt, and turquoise flip-flops. "You two are certifiable!"

I looked at Jamie, she looked at me, and we both looked at his hairy ankles.

"Tell him," I whispered. "He'll take it better coming from you."

Jamie took a deep breath. She walked into the bathroom, and came out with a pink Gillette razor and shaving cream. "Here." She held them out to Tom.

"No thanks. I don't shave yet," said Tom.

"Your legs. You have to shave your legs," said Jamie.

50

Tom looked down at his hairy ankles. He looked over at Jamie's legs. She was wearing khaki shorts, and her legs were brown and smooth.

Then he looked at my legs.

I was wearing yellow shorts, and my legs had too many scratches and scrapes and bumps and bruises to look tan and smooth, though it's a mystery to me how Jamie and I have spent practically every minute of every summer together for our whole lives, but her legs look like she's spent our entire summer vacation lying by a pool sipping smoothies in Hawaii and mine look like I've spent our entire summer vacation on my hands and knees pulling turnips from the garden behind Mrs. Lucky Pike's Burger Café.

"You guys are out of your minds if you think I'm shaving my legs and wearing a skirt and... these!" He threw the skirt, blouse, and flip-flops at me.

"Bagpipe players wear skirts." My attempted smile got stuck halfway up my right cheek.

"Olympic swimmers shave," Jamie pleaded.

"Then get a bagpipe playing Olympic swimmer to help you solve this case because I'd rather be thrown in jail and pounded by petnappers than shave my legs and wear a skirt."

"Hold on." I ran to my room to grab my backpack, then tore through my clothes again. "Here." I handed Tom an old pair of Levis, a navy blue t-shirt, a Cincinnati Reds baseball cap, and aviator sunglasses. "Clean clothes."

Tom slammed the bathroom door without another word, but that suited me just fine. Three days without a shower was not agreeing with that kid. If he still had to look like a boy, at least he didn't have to smell like one.

TEN

We hurried down our block on our way to the pet store. When we got to the corner of South "A" Street, I looked around to make sure no one was following us. The only living things in sight were an army of black ants scurrying in and out of their sandy sidewalk fortress and Mrs. Granger's old Persian curled up on a wicker rocking chair on her front porch.

"Guys, slow down." As we walked past the Loyal Order of the Loping Antelope Lodge, it occurred to me that we were drawing attention to ourselves by walking so fast, not that there was a single person outside whose attention we would draw. No one walks fast around here except my parents, but they're from New York City, and they really can't help themselves.

"It's just a few more blocks, anyway," Jamie said.

"You think the store will be locked? Or Mr. Humperdink will be there?" I asked Tom.

"Quick," Tom yanked my arm and Jamie's shirt, "behind the tree."

Lead weights must have dropped straight down from the cloudless sky into my sneakers because my feet wouldn't move a millimeter.

"Not here!" I panicked. This was Bartholomew Jackson's redbud tree in front of Bartholomew Jackson's house, which Bartholomew Jackson could have been inside of at that very moment looking out his picture window and thinking what a lovesick loser I was spying on him from his own front yard.

52

*   *   *

Bartholomew Jackson and I had been a hot number all last year, which basically meant that we never spoke to each other, never looked at each other, and never messaged each other. Our only actual semi-contact was on Valentine's Day, when he made Matthew Wormword give me his mushy, grown-up Valentine's Day card saying lots of stuff about flowers and feelings and passionate love. He signed it,

XXXXXXXOOOOOOO,
Bartholomew Jackson Alexander McGill

So I made Jamie give him my just-in-case mushy Valentine's Day card that I'd picked out in the Mushy-Card section of Phil's Pharmacy. I signed it,

XXXXXXXOOOOOOO,
Indiana Bamboo

Everyone knew we were a couple, which made me popular for the first time ever. I never knew how we became a couple. One day, it was just a fact. And just as mysteriously, two days before summer vacation, it was over.

Bartholomew Jackson never told me why he didn't love me anymore, which of course he wouldn't have since he hadn't talked to me once the whole year we were going out, and he wasn't likely to start the day he decided to break up with me. I found out when Ollie Eaton stomped up to me in the lunchroom, cleared his throat, and announced, loud enough for every single kid to hear over Snapple slurping and carrot crunching, "Bartholomew Jackson said to give you this message—'IT'S OVER.'"

And that was that. No more Bartholomew Jackson. No more popular.

I hadn't told anyone, not even Jamie, that my heart still did back handsprings every time I passed his house—not that it mattered because I was so totally over him, and the fact that my heart hadn't gotten the message was completely beside the point.

*   *   *

"It's them," Tom cried, interrupting my panic with his own.

"Indy, hurry." Jamie yanked my other arm so hard my elbow cracked, knocking the lead right out of my sneakers and Bartholomew Jackson right out of my brain.

A black panel truck was slowing down at the entrance to the Loyal Order of the Loping Antelope Lodge. The driver opened his window and spoke into the intercom, then the wrought iron gates swung open and he drove through, disappearing behind the curtain of elms that lined the drive.

We scooted across the street and scooched behind the limestone wall that surrounded the Lodge.

"Think this is electrified or anything?" Tom scratched his stringy blond hair.

"I think Indy's imagination is rubbing off on you. We used to play 'Capture the Flag' here all the time," Jamie said.

"C'mon." I rushed over the wall. "Ow!" I winced as my right knee hit the dirt.

"Are you okay?" Jamie scrambled over the wall and landed in a cushion of leaves that I could've sworn hadn't been there a second before.

"Duck!" Tom hissed in a loud whisper as he landed in that same cushion of leaves.

A messy-red-headed guy had suddenly appeared from around back. He pushed open the front door of the Lodge.

"Is that...?"

Tom nodded.

"How do you know it's not some other big, messy-red-headed guy riding in a black panel truck?" I asked.

A huge man with a brown buzz stuck his head out the doorway of the Loyal Order of the Loping Antelope Lodge as Messy-red-headed guy went inside. Then he looked around quickly and slammed the door.

We looked at each other, and for once, none of us said a word.

We knew what we had to do.

ELEVEN

My heart thumped in my ears as we zigged and zagged from tree to tree. We made it to the Lodge, climbed the steps to the front door and pushed. It didn't budge.

"Something's blocking the door," Tom whispered.

"I don't think so." Jamie began to bounce. "My dad takes us to brunch here every New Year's Day. It's a really heavy door."

"Messy-red-headed guy opened it like it was nothing." Tom turned pale as the ghost I'd thought he was.

"We can't think about that now." I gulped, though the thought of just how easily that Messy-red-headed guy could pound us if he could open that door like it was nothing made my ears pop. "Just push!"

We pushed and pushed.

"Again," I urged. "On the count of three. One, two—"

"ShhhRUP!" The door jerked open. We stumbled into the marble entranceway. Directly in front of us, a grand mahogany staircase spiraled up and up, and up some more.

Jamie raced up the stairs on tiptoes. We followed behind, cringing with every creak of the stairs. When we reached the top, I looked straight ahead and froze.

Tom stopped short beside me. A stuffed brown bear greeted us at the landing, its arms raised, claws out, and teeth bared.

"Maurice." I could barely whisper his name.

"No, no. That's Igor," said Jamie. "Poor guy's been here forever."

"Zee pleasure ees all mine, Igor." Tom bowed and shook the bear's paw.

Just as it registered in my brain that poor, old Igor looked about twice as big as Maurice, Jamie tugged my arm.

"In here," she ordered. A stained glass window in the shape of a leaping antelope cast an eerie amber glow into the dark room.

"AAARGH!"

Three sharp gasps pierced the silence, and one of them was mine. I put my hand across Tom's mouth, he put his on mine, and we each put a hand across Jamie's. Someone tall—and I mean, very tall—was watching us from the other side of the room. The whites of his eyes flashed as they followed our every move.

"Shhh! I hear something." I clasped my hand harder on Jamie's mouth to shush the raspy whimpering sound she was making.

Muffled voices echoed from the doorway leading to the back hall.

"Hurry!" said Jamie, shaking off my hand and shoving Tom and me behind the counter.

"Scrunch down!" I pointed to our shadowy reflections in the wide mirror above the bar.

Just inside the doorway to the back hall, Brown-buzz guy stood listening to a much shorter guy, with a shiny, bald head, who was talking up a storm. I closed my eyes to concentrate, but all I could hear was,

"...psssst, sssss, sssssssss, shhhhh, sss, sshhui, shhu, sssss, sssst, sshueeee, sss..."

My heart pounded so hard it hurt across my shoulders, up my neck, and through my ears. I pulled on Jamie's arm and was sliding along the wall when a gravelly voice cracked the silence. Brown-buzz guy's voice.

"We'll be there in—"

"Up here, Margaret," another voice—a woman's billowy, husky voice—boomed from the front hallway.

"Let's scram," Brown-buzz guy growled.

Jamie, Tom, and I dove back behind the bar, just as the woman flicked a switch, flooding the room with light.

"This little pub is perfect," she purred, walking out into the front hall.

I blinked back the brightness and squinted. Terrified, I looked around the room ready—well, breathing really, really fast and pretending to myself that I was ready—to face Messy-red-headed guy or whichever of Brown-buzz guy's sparkly-eyed accomplices was in here watching us. Then I saw him.

His head stared down at me, with those shiny eyes, but the rest of him was... I ordered my brain cells to freeze that instant because no way did I want to start imagining where the rest of him was.

The head of the poor fellow who'd been watching us was mounted on the wall, but he wasn't a fellow—not a human one, anyhow. He was a zebra. At least, he used to be. And the heads of his used-to-be zebra family were lined up biggest to smallest on the dark wood paneling next to him.

"Creepy," Tom murmured, staring back and forth between the lion's head roaring on one wall and the giraffe's head on another.

"That's the understatement of the century," I murmured back.

"The founder of Fabulous Flavours Pet Products—you know, Otto Flavours, the First—lived here. He left it to LOLA—the Loyal Order of the Loping Antelope—when he died," Jamie whispered.

"Weird—you'd think he would've liked animals if he started a pet food company. You think he's the one who hunted 'em?" Tom asked.

"I guess things were different way back then." Jamie shrugged.

"Listen, dears," the woman bellowed through the doorway, "we'll cover the bar for your little soiree. It will be divine.

The perfect eleventh birthday party." She clickety-clacked into the room with her shiny red high heels.

"You're kidding," Jamie gasped.

"Gimme a break," Tom mouthed.

"Gag me with a spoon." I stuck my index finger in my mouth for emphasis. I mean, for cryin' out loud, we're not talking Beverly Hills here. What kind of show-off would hire Mrs. LaGrande, River Creek's one and only part-time wedding planner, for an eleventh birthday party?

The answer to that question walked right through the door.

Autumn Winters. Autumn's mother, Mrs. Arabella Winters, younger sisters Summer and Spring, and four miniature mutts trailed behind her in perfect formation, tallest to smallest, noses in the air.

It figured. Ever since Autumn ratted me out in third grade for eating all the M&M's our teacher Miss Honeydew had brought in for the Math Bee—and left on her desk for two long days before I couldn't take it anymore—Autumn Winters has been my Lex Luther, my Professor Moriarty, my Draco Malfoy. Except for one thing.

She's not bad. She's good. Brown-nosingly, disgustingly good. She used to be just a sore pain in the you-know-where but now she really had me sizzling because eighteen-and-a-half seconds after Bartholomew Jackson broke up with me, she whipped her freeze-dried, pancake-flat hair around, kissed him smack on the lips in front of everyone in the lunchroom, and stole away any chance I had of getting him back.

Not that I'd wanted him back, of course, but it was the principle of the thing.

I looked at the door to the back hallway. Brown-buzz guy and Shiny-bald-headed guy were gone.

"We have to get out of here," I whispered, nodding toward the now empty doorway.

While Mrs. LaGrande chattered on and on about what a divine eleventh birthday party she would design, Jamie raised her finger to her lips and motioned for us to follow her. We slinked back along the bar to the storeroom door. Jamie pushed it open, and we ran.

"Hey, you!" someone yelled. Actually, two someones—a gravelly-voiced someone in one direction and a billowy, husky-voiced someone in the other.

We sped through the storeroom past shelves of glasses, into a narrow hallway which circled straight into... a dead end.

"This way." Jamie turned and kept running.

We followed her through the dining room, down the back stairs, and into the library. At least, I thought it was a library because it had one of those cool sliding ladder things, except I came this close to knocking over a model of the U.S.S. Constitution just like mine at home, and I looked around. The bookshelves were chock full of model ships.

"I could use a little help here!" Tom was trying to push open a window, but it was painted shut. Jamie and I climbed on top of a gigantic roll top desk, and banged the frame until the window popped open. I climbed out first and jumped.

"OW!" I wailed. You know the saying, 'Look before you leap?' One scrawny rosebush leaning against the building, and I had to land in it. I was starting to feel as beaten up as the eggs in the egg drop soup at Mrs. Chan's Chinese restaurant.

We bolted behind the shrubs at the side of the drive as Mrs. LaGrande, Autumn, and Autumn's entourage zoomed out the door, V-roomed the engine, and took off in Mrs. Winters' Jaguar.

"You okay?" Tom asked.

I let out a deep breath. "That was too close."

"We're not out of the soup yet. Where are Brown-buzz guy, Messy-red-headed guy, and that Shiny-bald-headed guy?" Jamie asked.

I peeked through the shrubs and saw... nothing.

The truck was gone.

TWELVE

"What's that?" I brushed off Jamie's shoulder. A red feather floated into Tom's outstretched palm.

"Hendrix!" He smiled with a great, big face-cracking smile. "Hendrix was here!"

"What do you mean was?" I asked. "Hendrix and the other animals could be hidden at the Lodge now!"

"No way." Jamie bopped up and down on her toes. "No way could they hide a whole store-load of animals without someone noticing something."

I grabbed the feather from Tom's hand and held it up to Jamie's face. "Oh yeah? Explain this!"

"That feather could have gotten there lots of ways, like on someone's clothes. Those men...," Jamie bounced faster and faster, shook her head, twirled her ponytails, and muttered, "huge... strong... coming back!"

With all her bravery at the Lodge, I'd thought she'd finally gotten over this muttering stuff.

"St--Stop!" Jamie ordered, as Tom and I walked to the front door. "We... need... to... call... the... police."

The cobblestones crackled, and an engine V-roomed. Man, I thought, can't any of these people drive without V-rooming their engines? We turned to see who was roaring up the lane.

Someone had called the police for us.

Officer Martin and Captain Rodriguez climbed out of the River Creek black-and-white squad car. Captain Rodriguez flipped open her police pad and started writing while Officer Martin sauntered over.

"Indiana, Jamie, and...?" Officer Martin inspected us from head to toe, and I swear, the instant his gaze landed on Tom's eyes, it was like someone took out a brush and painted disapproval all over his face. "Well, well, well. Which Weaver do we have here?"

"I'm Tom, sir."

"Following in your brother Cody's footsteps, are ya, Tom?"

"Cody didn't mean to..." As Officer Martin's eyes narrowed into a ferocious frown, Tom hastily added, "No, sir."

"He's not..."

"We were just..."

Jamie and I began at the same time, but Officer Martin shut us down with a fierce unibrow scowl.

"We just got three," he held up two thumbs and one index finger for emphasis, "anonymous calls from Mrs. Winters, Mrs. LaGrande, and some guy reporting three kids trespassing in the Lodge."

He stuck out that bony index finger until it nearly touched my nose and made my eyes cross. Pointing from one nose to the other, he counted, "One. Two. Three."

Then he crossed his arms in front of his chest, and waited.

"It wasn't us, Officer," I blurted.

Okay. I panicked. That wasn't exactly the plan. Lying to a police officer isn't high on my top ten list of smart things to do.

"5-4-3-2-1," I counted down in my head, waiting for Jamie to crack.

On cue, out of the silence, a voice began talking a mile a minute. "We're really, really sorry. We didn't know we were doing anything wrong. I mean, it's not actually trespassing if the door isn't locked—is it? We just wanted to see the bear and the animal heads and... and... are we in trouble?"

I let out a giant breath then my stomach did a triple axel when I realized—that was my voice talking.

Jamie looked at me in plain astonishment. Tom's face was turning a pretty angry looking shade of red.

Captain Rodriguez snapped her pad closed. Officer Martin paced back and forth. He shook his head, turned away, and paced some more. He must have done that for a whole minute before he began to talk, but once he did, he got himself so wound up that he paced faster and faster and talked louder and louder.

"Do you kids know how dangerous it is to snoop around like that?" He swept his arms through the air. "Maybe the floor could collapse. Maybe the place is guarded—GRRR," he growled, and we jumped back, "by attack dogs. Maybe next time you startle someone—Boom! They shoot first, ask questions later, like when you're dead."

Pictures danced across my brain of Mrs. LaGrande holding a squirt gun with her six inch nails while the Winters' frou-frou attack mutts yapped by her side. I almost forgot we were in the soup until Officer Martin reminded me.

"Forget dead." Officer Martin's eyes bulged and his cheeks puffed out so far a pinprick would have popped them. "In case you've forgotten," and it's true he's had to remind me once or twice in the past, "trespassing is against the law," he shouted in his usual delicate manner.

He leaned against the car, muttering to himself in genuine Jamie fashion. "Can't take the stress. Stupid kids. Gonna get themselves killed." He pulled out a handkerchief and wiped his forehead.

Captain Rodriguez took it from there. "This is your warning. Your only warning. Two strikes and you're out. We've got a pet store robbery to solve, and we can't waste time keeping you kids out of trouble. You throw a gum wrapper on the sidewalk, let those bikes of yours so much as touch the line inside a handicapped spot, jay walk across Main Street on a Sunday morning at six a.m., you're toast.

"And if we ever, and I mean EVER catch you trespassing here again, it's straight to the slammer! Do... I... make...

myself… clear?" She shook her police pad to emphasize each word.

"Yes, ma'am," we answered in unison.

"Then scram. Skedaddle! Go play on the playground!"

Thirteen

We skedaddled down Seventeenth Street toward Redbud, feeling the laser beam rays of Captain Rodriguez's eyes at our backs as we ran. Next thing we knew, we'd skedaddled straight into my backyard.

"That was close." Jamie collapsed under Fort Bamboo.

"No kidding!" Tom collapsed beside her.

"How long do you think until they're gone?" I asked.

"Who?" Jamie asked.

"Captain Rodriguez and Officer Martin," I said.

Jamie narrowed her eyes while raising her right eyebrow. "Did you already forget what Captain Rodriguez said three seconds ago? Or was that your zombie-alien, coconut-brained double standing next to me?"

I turned my zombie-alien coconut-brain on overdrive to think of a way around Captain Rodriguez and Officer Martin, not to mention those overgrown bad guys, but not one single idea crashed, floated, or hung around like a lazy day.

"Fine." I sighed, more than a little grumpily. "Back to Plan A—To Paradise Pets. But let's ride bikes this time." I walked to the garage and punched in the code. The automatic garage door whirred, then flipped up. "You can borrow one of Dad's," I said to Tom.

Tom's mouth fell open, but no words came out. My dad's inventions are like that gooey green glob in horror movies that oozes like lava, sucking up everything in its path, which is what Dad's broken, forgotten, and pieces of inventions do in every nook and cranny of our supersized, thirteen bay garage.

I poked around to find a bike for Tom that hadn't been turned into a soda fountain or Dad's Human Energy Recovery System, a.k.a., H.E.R.S.

"What's this?" Tom bent down to examine the H.E.R.S.

"Dad's latest attempt to harness energy from the ladies riding exercise bikes at Joy-Lynn's Bakery, Exercise Emporium, and Special Occasion Beauty Salon."

Tom climbed on and began pedaling.

"Right now," I pointed to the violet flashing lights on the console, "your energy is being stored in the teeniest, tiniest, super-duper powered batteries, but my dad's working on B.E.C.—the Bamboo Energy Cloud—to store energy in cyberspace."

"What the—!" Tom toppled off the bike and stifled a holler.

A creature creeping up from a rusty, claw-footed bathtub plopped down in the middle of Garage Bay Six. It looked like a fingerpainting gone wrong with white blotches covering its entire left side and humongous red splotches covering its entire right side—not to mention its orange bathing suit, blue flippers, and red snorkel mask.

"Dad!" I cried. "What happened?"

"Blurrrr." Dad knocked the water out of his ears and buzzed his lips, bearing a remarkable resemblance to the police horse, Old Blister. He took off his mask as he waddled in our direction. "Hey, there, kiddos."

"Mr. Bamboo, are you doing another poison ivy experiment?" Jamie raced up to Dad and stared as the red splotches grew bigger and splotchier.

"Never!"

Dad held up a thin, square towelette. "Introducing my latest variation on the *invisi-wipe*!" Then he rubbed it up and down his left arm, and opened his empty hands. "Ta Da!"

The towelette was gone.

"It's vanishing! It's biodegradable! It's the lean, green, INVISI-SUNSCREEN!"

"But what happened, Mr. Bamboo?" asked Jamie.

"Works like a charm in fresh or salt water, but dive into a swimming pool and," he scratched his arm, "you'll swim out with these itchy red blotches."

"While you're working, would you mind if Tom borrowed one of your bikes?" I asked.

"How do you do?" Dad noticed Tom for the first time and held out his right hand to shake. Then he remembered the red splotches and just nodded instead. His eyes sparkling, he added, "The Speed Demon—Bay Seven. Watch the brakes in seventy-sixth gear and you'll be A-Okay."

"Thanks." Tom nodded back, then nodded some more. "Nice to meet you, sir."

"Well, back to the old drawing board." Dad put on his mask, waddled the few steps to the tub, and bubbled back down into the water.

"Seventy-sixth gear?" Tom asked.

"It's got ninety-nine." I wheeled the Speed Demon over to Tom.

"Cool." Tom gripped the handlebars, but a teeny, tiny, "Is-this-bike-going-to-explode-into-a-bijillion-pieces-in-seventy-sixth-gear?" dot of doubt twitched just above his upper lip.

I recognized it straight away. I've had my own teeny, tiny dot of doubt, too—except mine's more like, "Is this the time Dad's going to morph me into an artichoke?"

Jamie hopped on her Black Bomber, and I hopped on my Red Ranger.

"Listen," said Tom, as we rode to Paradise Pets, "Mr. H.'s spare key is buried in the second hydrangea to the left of the front door. I'll meet up with you guys later."

Jamie stopped riding. "Where are you going?"

"You can't ditch Paradise Pets forever." I stopped next to Jamie, which happened to be right in front of Hanrahan's Department Store.

Crossing my fingers six ways for good luck, I peeked inside, but no sign of Mom buying me a Surprise-Hanrahan's-Tween-Training-So-You-Won't-Be-The-Lamest-Sixth-Grader-In-The-Locker-Room-At-Martin-Memorial-Middle-School-Birthday-Bra.

"That's not it—I swear. I just need to check on—check in at home," said Tom, as I took one more peek through the store window.

"Then we're coming with you," Jamie insisted.

"You don't have to," said Tom.

"And let you face Brown-buzz and Messy-red-headed guys alone? No way!" I said.

"We'll be your lookouts just like we planned," said Jamie.

"Don't you have to get home or something?" Tom asked.

Actually, I did. Absent-minded though my parents are, they've never in my whole entire life forgotten my birthday. Then a thought that had been hiding out in the corners of my brain escaped from my mouth.

"Would you like to come? To my birthday party?"

Tom hesitated.

I blushed.

Jamie swooped in for the rescue. "You have to come! You haven't tasted real birthday cake until you've tried one of Mrs. Bamboo's concoctions."

"And Mom even promised to let up on spinach, cauliflower, and the evil Brussels sprouts in the batter, on account of its being my birthday," I added. "We can stop at your house on the way."

Tom shrugged and nodded. "Okay. Sure."

"What are we waiting for?" I said. "Let's go!"

FOURTEEN

We rode down Southeast Avenue, Jamie muttering the entire time about crazy, lunatic drivers. First chance we had, we cut into James Whitcomb Riley Park.

I practically sprained my neck turning every which way to find the black panel truck, but the park was quiet. Just trees, grass, and a couple of teenagers making out on the bench beside Lover's Lake.

Tom stopped short. Jamie nearly toppled off her bike. She looked like a lightning bolt had slashed through the sky and zapped her right on the spot.

"That's your sister." Tom ducked behind the statue of the Madonna of the Trail.

"With your brother." Jamie didn't take her eyes off Elizabeth and Cody as she followed Tom.

"Kissing." I wrinkled my nose.

"It's...," Jamie began.

"Gross," I said.

"Perfect," Tom said at the same time, a lopsided smile pushing its way across his face.

"Excellent." Jamie grinned, looking like the cat who'd gulped the canary, which reminded me of my cats who absolutely, positively had not gulped P.J., but the thought of poor P.J. made my stomach flip sideways all over again.

"They look busy," I said.

"They look busted," Tom said.

"Sibling blackmail. It's a beautiful thing." Jamie said, still grinning.

"Earth to Jamie. Have you lost your mind? Don't you think," and I couldn't believe I was saying this, "you... shouldn't you tell your parents?"

"It's not like they're in danger." Jamie scooted her bike forward until she was next to Elizabeth.

I wasn't so sure about that. With their faces all smashed together and their arms wrapped around each other like octopuses, Cody and Elizabeth looked to me like they were in mortal danger of suffocation.

Jamie hopped off her bike. She put her hands on her hips and stood practically on top of Elizabeth. Tom pulled up and stood beside her.

Elizabeth and Cody didn't budge. They were too busy locking lips.

A full thirty seconds went by before Jamie said, "Hello, Elizabeth."

"Hey, Cody." Tom smirked as Cody and Elizabeth jumped straight up in the air.

"What the heck?" Cody said.

"If you tell, I'll...," Elizabeth began at the same time.

"No worries," Jamie said.

"No problem." Tom opened his arms, raising both hands.

Then he and Jamie hopped back on their bikes, and we rode off.

"Cody'll drive us. Any time. Any place. No questions asked," Tom said.

"It's a done deal," Jamie agreed.

And out of the blue, I felt it.

The Pang.

The vague—okay, not so vague—longing for a sister. Or brother. Either one would do. Not for sibling blackmail, but for all the stuff Jamie and Tom complain about and don't realize how lucky they are to have.

But just as The Pang was settling deep down in the pit of my stomach to stay a while, we turned onto a tree-lined block.

"This is it." Tom motioned to a small, white house just off the corner.

The little front yard shimmered. It was a jungle of color, with red, white, peach, yellow, and lavender rose bushes, lilacs and tulips, and gazillions of other flowers whose names I never could remember.

A life-size plastic pink flamingo was perched on a rock in a tiny lily pond. It was perfect, though in my opinion, you never can have too many pink flamingoes. Unfortunately, my parents don't agree, but I just have to keep reminding myself that when it comes to—more or less everything—they're from New York, and they really—really—can't help themselves.

"It's—"

"Paradise." Jamie finished my sentence.

"My mom and dad... My mom loved... loves gardening." Tom sounded kind of nervous as he added, "I'd better get going."

"Okay." I looked around the corner and up the street. "Jamie and I will keep a lookout for Messy-red-headed and Brown-buzz guys."

"I'll be back in a few minutes," said Tom.

We took up our posts, me behind the maple tree at the corner, Jamie crouched behind the fence at the side of the house. Tom walked the Speed Demon around back so he could climb in the hidden window.

After five minutes, I began to wonder how different living in a house with five boys felt from living in a house like Jamie's with five girls—minus all the hairdryers and guinea pigs and stuff. After ten minutes, I began to wonder if his house was as pretty on the inside as it was on the outside. After fifteen minutes, when there was no one in sight except Pete from Pete's Precise Plumbers, I couldn't wait for another second to find out.

"Jamie," I whispered. "Jamie!"

"Shhhh." She motioned me back.

"Just taking a teeny peek." I edged closer. "For all we know, they have a roller coaster in there."

"Don't be ridiculous, Indy. Go back!"

I crept around to the hidden window, squeezed behind a giant rhododendron bush, and squinted inside. No sign of a roller coaster, but Mrs. Weaver was lying on the couch in the den staring straight ahead. The TV wasn't on, so I couldn't figure out what she was looking at. Tom walked in, and I dove to the ground.

Not fast enough. He spotted me, and dropped the teacup in his hand.

A second later, he was at the back door.

"I'm sorry," I began, brushing dirt off my legs. "I just wondered what was taking so long. The street was real quiet and no one drove by except Pete and... does your mom have a migraine? I always make my mom chamomile tea when she has a migraine. Well, she's never had a real migraine, but she had a bad headache once from not eating on Yom Kippur—that's a Jewish holiday, but... um... I guess you already knew that. Anyhow—"

"Listen," Tom interrupted, clearly not focused on the fact that I'd been spying—or anything I'd been saying, for that matter, "what if Brown-buzz and Messy-red-headed guys come looking for me, and my mom's all alone? I'd better stay here and skip your birthday party."

The thought of anyone being alone with those guys, especially Brown-buzz guy, made my heart leap in terror. Heck, I'll bet Brown-buzz guy's heart leaps in terror when he's all alone with himself.

"Here." I slapped my cell phone into Tom's hand. "Keep it. You might have to call 911."

"Thanks, but we have phones."

"Oh... right. Well, keep one close in case you need it. We'll come get you to go to Paradise Pets first thing in the morning."

I started to leave, then turned back. "And lock the windows," I added. "Especially that back one."

"We'll be fine. For once, it feels good to be home."

And for once, I didn't ask him why.

Fifteen

The next morning, I was fast asleep on my bunk in Fort Bamboo, dreaming that I'd turned into a tap dancing torti- lla stuffed with sour cream, guacamole, and Chocolate Mon- soon Madness birthday cake. Purple lights above the bay window flashed, "HAPPY BIRTHDAY INDIANA! HAPPY BIRTHDAY INDIANA! HAPPY BIRTHDAY INDIANA!" while Mom, Dad, Lyle, and Jamie yelled, "Happy Birthday, Indiana! Open your eyes!"

Just like they did at my party.

Except they wouldn't stop shouting.

"Open your eyes! Open your eyes!"

I covered my ears. My heart was pounding harder than the entire drum brigade of the River Creek High School marching band. I didn't know if I was asleep or awake.

The little hairs on my arms shivered as a creepy feeling crept into my dream. Someone was staring down at me, but I couldn't tell how big a someone it was, and I didn't especially want to find out.

I swallowed hard and forced my eyes open, ready to face the music.

"Indiana, open your eyes!"

"Ahhhh!" I screamed, then realized that those narrowed eyes staring down at me were a familiar shade of gray.

"Ahhhh! Ooooww!" Jamie screamed as she bolted up in the bunk below me and clonked her head. "What are you doing here so early?"

"You could have given us heart attacks," I snapped.

"You're too young to get heart attacks," said Tom. "And, you're late. It's after eleven. You were supposed to pick me up first thing in the morning. Remember?"

"It can't be after eleven," I yawned. "I never sleep past six thirty."

"You really oughta' get some security around here. You guys didn't even hear me climb up."

"We have security."

I slapped my forehead. "Ah, man." I couldn't believe it. Bad guys on the loose, and I'd forgotten to pull up the rope ladder last night.

I handed Tom a cup of Grape Guts and a huge piece of Chocolate Monsoon Madness cake, then cut slices for Jamie and me.

"Thanks," said Tom as he settled into the cornstalk recliner.

"Don't get too comfortable," I said. "Ready or not, we're going to Paradise Pets, and that means you, Tom Weaver."

"Onnn ooo ave ooo anngge?" he mumbled, his mouth crammed full of cake.

"What?" asked Jamie.

"Aaaanngge." He pointed to our purple flannel pajama pants and pink shirts with "HAPPY BIRTHDAY, INDIANA!" written in silver glitter across the front.

"Oh—right!" said Jamie.

"Don't move!" I shook the cake in my hand at Tom. "We'll be back in a flash."

Before you could say Chocolate Monsoon Madness, we'd run to my room, changed into t-shirts and shorts, and were racing out the kitchen door.

"Hang on." I stopped and turned around. "I'll be right back."

I rushed upstairs, filled up P.J.'s food bowl, and shoved it into the mouse hole in my room. I'd had this idea overnight that maybe, just maybe, I could lure P.J. out of the wall, if she'd nibble—

"Indy! Come on!" Jamie called.

Tom was scrambling down the rope ladder as we hurried into the backyard. We grabbed our bikes and started riding downtown to Paradise Pets.

"I've been wondering," I looked longingly at Stefano Stefano's as we zipped past, cravings for double chocolate Oreo and blueberry-peppermint crunch invading my stuffed-as-a-tortilla stomach, "do you think the police suspect Mr. Humperdink of rigging his own robbery?" Ever since Lyle had mentioned the inside job thing, that thought had stuck itself deep inside my brain, and I couldn't shake it away.

"In movies, it's always for the insurance money," said Jamie.

"Captain Rodriguez and Officer Martin have to know he'd never do that," Tom protested.

"But it said in the paper," and I lowered my voice to sound all grown-up and official, "'The police have not ruled out anyone as a suspect.'"

"Yeah." Tom frowned. "Like the mystery caller."

"Oh no." Jamie pointed to the squad car in the lot behind Paradise Pets. "Speaking of police...?"

We parked our bikes behind the dumpster. Jamie and I inched toward the store entrance so we could peek in. Tom hung back near the bikes. Suddenly, Jamie stopped cold.

"Jamie?" I turned to face her.

"I can't do it, Indy. I can't face Officer Martin and Captain Rodriguez again. I know I'll crack and start blathering the whole story if they so much as look at me. I've never been on the wrong side of the law before."

"But I'm the one who cracked at the Lodge, not you," I said, "and I'm not cracking again."

"If they catch us, there's no way they'll believe us now. They're gonna say it's Strike Two, and we're," Jamie gulped, "toast, and they'll throw us in the... slammer."

"Oh, for cryin' out loud," I said, "it's just Paradise Pets. We come here all the time!"

Jamie was glued to the pavement. I was on my own.

I hesitated for a second, then walked straight up to the window and looked inside. The store looked even more forlorn today than it had on Saturday, like emptiness had seeped into every corner and was settling in for good. I turned the doorknob. The door creaked open. I guess there wasn't much point in keeping the store locked, with all the animals gone.

"Hello?" I called. The cowbell clanged and echoed as I walked inside. "Anyone here? Mr. Humperdink? Captain Rodriguez?"

Taking "Mother May I" baby steps, I tiptoed to the storeroom where Tom had been sleeping the night the robbers came. My legs felt heavy, and I got this sick feeling as I stretched out my arm, opened the door, and croaked out a whispery, "Anybody in—"

"V-room!" My knees buckled. My stomach lurched. I hobbled over to the window and looked out. For some inexplicable reason, Officer Martin revved and revved the squad car engine while Captain Rodriguez wobbled into the passenger seat, balancing two giant bags of Chan's Chinese take-out.

"Jamie, Tom," I called in a stage whisper the second the police car V-roomed away. "Come quick! Captain Rodriguez has enough food to feed a platoon. We should have at least an hour to look around."

"This is bad." Tom walked to the doorway. "I never focused on how sad the store looked after it was cleaned out. I just wanted to get help for Mr. H."

Jamie checked over her shoulder to make sure the officers were really gone, and then walked inside. "It sure doesn't look promising for clues."

"Well, it's not like they're going to pop up and wave at us. We have to scour the place," I said.

We fanned out through the aisles. Except for the back where Maurice, Lily, and Esmerelda lived when they weren't outside in the habitat, the store felt a lot smaller empty than it had when it was filled with animals.

Tom climbed on the counters and began searching the top shelves. "No clues up here except a few de-worming pills."

I stared at one of the empty cages for a long minute. "I know puppies don't love being cooped up all day, but this is so... bare."

"That's weird." Tom shook his head. "There's dog food scattered around in that cage."

"What's so weird about that?" I asked.

"Mr. H. never overfeeds the animals. If any food's left over, he takes it away."

"Maybe he didn't have a chance to before he got conked," Jamie said.

"But that was at midnight. We feed the animals at six o'clock, on the dot. Mr. H is strict about everything—their breeders, their food, their—"

"Do you guys think," Jamie interrupted, "I mean... does either of you know... if maybe, somehow their food was... drugged?"

"Jamie—you're a genius," I cried, throwing my arms around her.

"Brilliant!" Tom reached down to slap her high five. "That's got to be it."

"Get all the stuff you can find." I began pacing around the store. "Food, water, bowls. We have to get it analyzed. It could be important evidence."

I was just taking a bowl out of a cage to put in my backpack when I heard a car door slam. I looked out the window.

The police were back. I guess they weren't that hungry after all.

Sixteen

I ran to the front of the store, grabbing Jamie.

"They're back—the police—let's go."

Tom hopped off the counter, and we tore outside, racing around the block to River Creek Community Theater. I slid down the wall and collapsed on the sidewalk.

"What happened to 'for cryin'... out loud... it's just Paradise Pets?'" Jamie collapsed next to me.

"I'm glad we got out of there." Tom leaned against the stage door as he spoke.

I wiped the sweat off my cheeks and caught my breath for a minute. "When the police came back, it felt like Strike Two. I figured Tom would get in big trouble for sure, and I just... sort of..." panicked, I thought, as my voice trailed off. The thing is, I never panic. Not ever.

Except I just had. Twice. In two days. Which was two times too many.

I looked down at my arms, my legs, and my bony knees, just to make sure I hadn't been replaced by some wimpy imitation me, but it was me, all right. A new, definitely not improved, gutless version of me that was out of here starting now.

Suddenly, I was famished. "Is anyone else hungry?"

"Starving," said Jamie. "How about Chan's?"

"Yeah. We won't bump into the police there considering that they already ordered everything on the menu," I said.

Jamie looked at Tom who was looking down. "It's on me. Well, on my parents, really. We're all nuts for Chinese food."

"Can you eat there whenever you want?" Tom asked, and I could practically see how big his smoky gray Weaver eyes got under his sunglasses.

"Naw. Just once a week. So, you wanna go?"

"Yeah. Thanks. I didn't have much money on me when I left Thursday night, so I haven't eaten anything in the last few days except the birthday cake and," Tom gave me a half-mischievous, half-guilty, half-smile, "a bunch of bananas and a couple of apples I nicked from your kitchen table. I guess Chan's should be pretty safe."

"It'll be empty by now. We're too early for dinner and too late for lunch." I half-smiled back.

We sneaked down the block to the rear entrance of Chan's.

I took a good look at Tom. "Keep your hat and sunglasses on. I'll go first to make sure the coast is clear."

"Hello, Indiana. How are you?" Mrs. Chan greeted me. She was wearing one of her elegant, red suits.

"Fine, thank you. There will be three of us, Mrs. Chan." I stayed close to the doorway to scope out the joint, then motioned to Jamie and Tom.

"It's completely empty. Except for them." I pointed to the lobsters creeping and crawling laps around the tank, unaware that these lumbering laps could be their last.

Mrs. Chan handed us menus as we sat at a table near the back door. "Do you kids know what you'd like?" She looked at Tom an extra second or two, but she didn't ask him to take off his hat. She must have decided he was covering up a bad haircut or something.

Before she had her pencil out of her apron, Tom answered, "Sweet and sour chicken and a Coke, please, and two egg rolls—if that's okay." He glanced over at Jamie, who smiled.

"We're all really hungry, Mrs. Chan," she said. "I'll have an egg roll, wonton soup, and fried dumplings, please."

"And for you, Indiana?"

"Egg drop soup, vegetable fried rice, and fruit punch. Thank you, Mrs. Chan."

"Wow. No one's ever known my name in a restaurant," Tom said, "but we only eat out on special occasions because my parents say the five of us boys eat so much we put the Indianapolis Colts to shame."

I wasn't sure what to say. I mean, it's not like Chan's is some chi chi restaurant in Cincinnati. It's good old Chan's in River Creek, Indiana, where everybody knows everybody else—or at least knows their brother or cousin or Great Aunt Hilda.

I pulled a plastic container full of critter kibble and a bowl from my backpack and put them on the starched white table-cloth. "I got this food and this bowl."

"Be careful with that stuff." Jamie reached over to keep the food from spilling. "For all we know, those poor animals were poisoned."

"Oh no." I panicked. "Princess Penelope!"

"And that cute little guinea pig—Teacup!" Jamie's face fell as she realized what she'd just said.

"And..." Maurice, I thought, but I couldn't bring myself to say his name out loud.

"Nah." Tom twirled the bowl in his hands. "What's the point of petnapping a bunch of poisoned animals?"

My stomach stopped its flips of fear. Jamie let out a deep breath then opened the huge Paradise Pets shopping bag she'd been holding.

"I took these." She pulled Esmerelda's giant food bowls from the bag.

Tom pulled two plastic bags out of his pockets, one with bird seed, and the other with guinea pig food. "There wasn't—"

"Autumn!" said Jamie. "Hi."

"Hi, Jamie." Autumn walked over from the cash register to our table.

I shoved the food and bowls into my backpack and under the table.

"Hello, Indiana. Hi... um..." Autumn flipped her freeze-dried, pancake-flat hair over her shoulder as her eyes flickered past Tom to the empty fourth seat next to Jamie.

"You don't want to lose your place in the take-out line, Autumn." I fake smiled. "Ow!"

Jamie kicked me under the table as she looked across the empty restaurant to the empty take-out line, but I didn't care. No way was Autumn-tattletale, steal-my-boyfriend Winters sitting with us. Besides, we had work to do.

"What's all that?" Autumn pointed to my backpack.

"All what?" I blinked.

"Just pet food," said Jamie, giving me the evil eyebrow. I sat on my legs lickety split. I could feel another kick coming.

"Autumn?" Mrs. Chan called. "Your order is all set, dear."

"Thank you, Mrs. Chan," she said in the sickly-sweet voice she saves just for grown-ups. "See you, Jamie."

As soon as Autumn walked out the door, Tom said, "Do you think she'll figure out what we're up to? Esmerelda's bowls are hard to miss."

"She's not going to worry about a little pet food. She's too busy thinking about her 'divine' eleventh birthday party." And being all kissy-face with Bartholomew Jackson Alexander McGill, I thought.

Rose, our waitress, arrived and set our tray on the wooden stand next to our table.

"Oh man, the smell of fried rice is making me even hungrier. Nothing smells as good as Chinese food," Jamie said.

"Except hot fudge," I added, "or guacamole."

I flopped under the table to get Esmerelda's bowls so Jamie could put them away in her bag, then we dug in. Jamie used chopsticks. I tried for a while, but I was too hungry for the struggle.

"So," Tom began, after we'd eaten in silence for a few minutes, not counting all our chewing, gulping, and a little too much slurping, "how're we going to get this stuff analyzed?"

"How about the FBI? Their labs are amazing. I saw this movie...," I began.

"The FBI?" Tom turned pale.

Jamie rolled her eyes. "Mr. Wilson—you know, the chemistry teacher at River Creek High—he'd do it."

"Can we trust him not to tell?" asked Tom, as Rose brought our fortune cookies.

"Heck yeah," I said. "He's the only person I've ever met who's more absent-minded than my parents. The guy's got a herd of llamas, about a million sheep..."

"...and so many kids, his family fielded their own softball team at the Future Farmers of America barbecue last spring!" added Jamie.

I nodded and munched my fortune cookie.

"What's it say?" asked Jamie.

"Good fortune comes to those who help themselves," I read, while Tom smashed open his cookie on the white tablecloth.

"Hey, that's some big fortune." I watched him unfold the paper.

"It's handwritten," Tom said.

"Handwritten?" Jamie leaned closer to get a better view. "I'll bet you won a prize!"

"Let's see." I started to grab it, but Tom snatched it back.

"Here goes." He read,

"KIDS WHO POKE NOZES WHERE NOT BEELONG TOODAY FIND NOZES IN FRYED RICE TOOMORO. BUTT OUT OR ELSE!"

Seventeen

Jamie was the first to speak, if you could call the words she croaked out of her throat actual speaking.

"I don't think you won a prize. We need to leave. Now!"

"It looks like Mrs. Chan is in on this, too." Tom's whole body slumped.

"No way. Mrs. Chan is not a thief. And besides, that fake fortune is spelled wrong. She would never be so careless. I'm going to talk to her right now."

"Indiana, no. Let's get out of here!" said Tom.

I pretended not to hear and strode up to Mrs. Chan. Whoever wrote that fortune must have sneaked in while we were eating. Which meant they were spying on us. Which so totally creeped me out I pushed the thought out of my brain.

"Mrs. Chan?"

"Yes, Indiana? How was lunch today?"

"Great as usual, thank you, but... our friend got kind of a strange fortune."

"Don't worry, dear. You mustn't take them seriously. They're just for fun, you know."

"No, I mean, his fortune—it was handwritten."

"Handwritten?" Mrs. Chan frowned as I looked over at Jamie and Tom. Jamie was twirling her ponytails and bouncing, Tom was twisting his left earlobe, and they were both motioning like crazy to hurry. I felt my nerve draining away.

"I'm kind of in a rush, and... um... I wondered if you noticed anyone unusual come into the kitchen while we were eating?"

"No, it's quiet now, just Rose and me. The kitchen help should be back any minute to prepare the vegetables for dinner."

"You didn't see anyone at all?" I blurted.

"No dear." She shook her head. "Just us, and the new delivery man."

"Delivery man?"

"He had a large shipment of tea, spices, and nuts, but we got that delivery yesterday. It was a mix up at the warehouse. It happens." She shrugged and smiled.

"Did he come inside?"

"Yes, he asked to use the restroom, and ordered three quarts of hot and sour soup, four spring rolls, six egg rolls, General Tso's chicken, beef lo mein, pork fried rice, and a small Diet Coke. He was a big fellow." She motioned to the ceiling.

"To go?" I asked, with a lump in my throat.

"At first. Then he asked if I'd mind if he ate in the kitchen. He said it had been a long day, and he would appreciate a few moments to rest. Very polite man. Even offered to pay."

My stomach turned into a giant knot. "Is he still in there?" I squeaked, nodding toward the kitchen, but the human mind is so weird.

While I was becoming officially terrified, I wondered if delivery guys always got free food.

"No, no. He left as soon as he finished eating."

The knot in my stomach untied itself.

"Mrs. Chan, did you see what was in his truck?"

"No dear, I already told you. It was a mix-up."

Mrs. Chan is one of the most patient adults I know, but by the way she was tapping her fingers on the cash register, I could tell I was pushing it.

"Just one more thing. What color was the... the new guy's hair?"

"Very bright hair. Bright red. Anything else, Indiana? You are full of questions today, but I must get back to work. Perhaps I should take a look." She reached for the glasses hanging around her neck and held out her hand for the fortune.

"Um... that's okay," I replied in my new falsetto voice, closing my fist around the fortune. "Thank you, Mrs. Chan. I have to go now."

I ran over to Jamie and Tom. "It was Messy-red-headed guy."

Before I could squeak out another word, Jamie grabbed my left arm and Tom grabbed my right. We were halfway out the front door when we froze.

A black panel truck crept along the street toward the entrance to the restaurant. I couldn't see the driver's face, but I could see his hair. His very bright, red hair.

Like New York City Rockettes, we spun around at exactly the same time and took flying leaps back inside. As I leapt, my cell phone knocked against my hip bone and fell.

"Quick, Indy, get a picture of the license plate." Jamie picked up my phone and handed it to me.

I stared at the phone in my hands.

"What are you waiting for?" Jamie asked as the truck crept closer.

"I don't know how," I said, and inside that second, my face got all hot, and I wanted to crawl under one of Mrs. Chan's tables. I must be the only kid in all of River Creek who wasn't born with natural cell phone instincts.

"Give it here." Jamie snatched my phone and started clicking. "My older sisters' cell phones are practically Krazy-glued to their ears," she said, "but I sneak them away every chance I get to play games."

"I can't see the license plate." Tom looked over Jamie's shoulder. "The pictures are too small."

"We'll check them out on Indy's computer in Fort Bamboo," said Jamie.

"C'mon." I began walking out the door.

"Watch out! He's doubling back!" Jamie cried.

"He must have seen us," Tom said.

"This way!" I ducked inside, pushed open the swinging door to the kitchen, and—

"Oouch! Hey!" The door crashed into the tray in Rose's hands, which clanked and clattered as it flipped, sending two doomed lobsters clawing through the air and a mound of bean sprouts spraying across the room.

"What's going on in there?" Mrs. Chan yelled to Rose and the two cooks chopping vegetables in the kitchen.

"We're sorry...."

"We'll make it up to you...."

"We promise," each of us called at the same time.

We brushed the bean sprouts off our clothes as we raced out of the kitchen, through the back door into the alley, and all the way around "B" Street into Readmore. We didn't stop until we sank into beanbag chairs in the "Fix My Teenage Life" section at the back of the bookstore.

"We have to get to Mr. Wilson's... analyze... food... and bowls," Jamie panted.

"We have to... follow... truck," I panted back. "He could be going to their hideout!"

"Indiana, in case you've forgotten, we don't drive," Jamie said.

"We'll ride fast on our bikes. Maybe he'll make other deliveries," I replied.

"Deliveries? That wasn't...," Tom began, gulping breaths, "a delivery. Messy-red-headed guy followed us to the restaurant."

"How could he have followed us? We haven't seen him since yesterday at the Lodge," Jamie said, picking bean sprouts out of my braids.

"How am I supposed to know how, but he followed us, didn't he?" said Tom. "That fortune didn't write itself."

I pushed Jamie's hands away from my braids. "We're wasting time. You guys can stay here and argue until Jupiter aligns with Mars, but I'm following that truck."

"And do what when you catch it? It's too dangerous."
Jamie frowned, but I didn't answer. I glanced down the street
to the left and right. The coast was clear. I began to run.

"Indiana Bamboo, you have about as much sense as a coconut! Those guys…"

I didn't hear the rest of what Jamie was shouting. I kept
running until I reached the Lionel Library, sprinted up the
stairs, and looked out the picture window in the third floor
magazine department.

I could see all of downtown River Creek, from Joy-Lynn's
Bakery, Exercise Emporium, and Special Occasion Beauty Salon, to Lucky's Burger Café, to the genuine, fifteen foot tall
replica of Michelangelo's sculpture of David peeking out from
the twenty foot dome in the ceiling of Lyle's ETCETERA.

But I was too late. The truck was gone.

Jamie and Tom were nowhere in sight, either, but I didn't
care. I was mad at Jamie anyhow. I stomped down the stairs
and bumped into Mrs. Ross, the librarian, on her way up.

"May I help…?" she whispered, raising her finger to her
lips to shush me.

"Sorry, my mistake," I whispered back.

I tiptoed out thinking how good a peanut butter cup
would taste just about now. Then it hit me. We hadn't talked
to the one person who knew more about the robbery than
anyone else.

It was time to visit Mr. Humperdink.

Eighteen

"Another long face? You look bluer than the Mediterranean sea on a cloudless day."

"Hi, Lyle."

"What can I do for you today, Indiana?" Lyle reached behind the counter to hand me the one-size-fits-all hot pink down parka.

"I'm going to visit Mr. Humperdink in the hospital, and I wondered if you have any suggestions for what I could bring him."

Then I noticed a new sign taped to the refrigerator case in the back:

We Now Carry Stefano Stefano's

Homemade Mexican Food

Featuring------>

Fresh Salsa, Tortillas and Beans, and Guacamole!

"I think just bringing yourself will cheer him up, but if you'd like—"

"Tortillas and Beans!"

"No, I don't think—"

"Guacamole...."

My eyes glazed over as the mouth-watering platter of tortillas and beans heaped with mounds of guacamole, sour cream, and fresh salsa that Lyle brought to my party yesterday filled the entire movie screen in my brain.

"Indiana... Indiana?"

"Huh?"

"Mr. Humperdink doesn't go for guacamole, but he is partial to papayas."

"Mr. Humperdink? Oh. Right. I'll take one papaya, and these." I held up the Reese's Peanut Butter Cups in my hand.

"That'll be three-fifty."

I searched my pockets and pulled out the same old crumpled dollar bill that I'd had Saturday. Dang. I knew I'd forgotten something. "Um... Do you think I could..."

"Well, isn't this a remarkable coincidence?" Lyle tossed me the papaya. "It's Birthday Dollar Deal Day! Buy one pack of peanut butter cups and get a papaya free!"

"Thank you, Lyle. Thank you so..."

Hang on a minute.

Lyle just sold me a papaya?

I stared at Lyle for a too-long second, then searched for the sign. It was still there, taped to the refrigerator case where it had been forever:

Special Orders Accepted for Everything
Except
YOU KNOW WHAT!

Though he didn't say another word, the look in Lyle's eyes as he pretended to straighten some doo-dad or other was as if he was telling me the story all over again, at least as much of the story as I'd ever heard.

"Her name," he'd always begin, "was Yvette. Eee-vet-tay," he'd say, emphasizing each syllable to be sure that there was no mistake about it.

"Every day at two cups of coffee past dawn, when the first ray of the first sunbeam of the morning warmed her soft, copper skin until it shone like a new penny, she'd sit at her whitewashed kitchen table, the one with the one leg shorter than the other three, and begin to slice the papay..."

And here, every single time, his voice would crack, and his words would evaporate, like the ribbons of steam drifting up from her coffee, into the silence. But if you looked real quick, at just the right instant, you might just catch Eee-vet-tay's sweet, sad smile deep inside Lyle's glistening brown eyes.

My heart would ache just looking at him. I knew there was no happily ever after, because Eee-vet-tay was—well, I didn't know where Eee-vet-tay was because I'd never heard the end of the story. All I knew for sure was that she wasn't here with Lyle, who was standing all alone behind the counter of the ETCETERA, just like he had for every single day of my whole entire life.

Lyle looked up and cleared his throat. "Tell Mr. Humperdink I'll be over to see him after closing time."

"I will." I peeled off the pink parka. "Thank you, Lyle."

And I realized, as I walked out, how lucky Mr. Humperdink was to have a friend like Lyle.

I walked back to Paradise Pets to get my bike. It was behind the dumpster where I'd left it, but I got a funny feeling in the pit of my stomach when I saw that Jamie and Tom's bikes were gone.

I rode to the River Creek Memorial parking lot, glad to ditch the Danica Patrick wannabe's zooming like maniacs on Southeast Avenue. Who needs Jamie and Tom anyhow, I thought, as I walked into the lobby and strode up to the information desk like I did this every day.

"I'm looking for Mr. Humperdink."

"Are you a relative?" The guard scowled.

"Yes. I'm his uncle. I mean, he's my niece."

The guard rolled his eyes, and motioned to the elevator. "Fourth floor, first left. Room 454." He didn't even blink at the papaya.

The elevator doors opened. I crinkled my nose, trying not to breathe in the cloud of disinfectant soaking the air. As I stepped into the hallway, someone yanked on my arm, but before I could karate chop the culprit, I realized there were two culprits. Jamie and Tom.

"Shhh." Tom pulled me to the corner where Jamie stood, not looking at me.

"What are you two doing here?" I asked, trying to make my voice as icy as the strawberry smoothie I'd had last week, the one that gave me the worst brain freeze ever.

"Same as you." Tom looked from me to Jamie. "You two are going to have to be mad later. The nurse will be back any second. It's now or never."

With Tom in the middle, we hurried on tiptoes to Room 454. Lined up like three bobbleheaded dolls, we peered around the open door.

Mr. Humperdink was sitting up in bed in his electric blue hospital gown, eating some neon orange, gloopy-looking stuff that I'm guessing was mashed potatoes and gravy in a previous life. I was relieved to see that he didn't have any tubes stuck in his arms, but he did have a heavy-duty mummy theme going on with white bandages wrapped all around his head. That must have been some bad conk.

He began talking to someone. I leaned in to see who it was, except I tripped sideways and pushed Tom. Tom stumbled into the room, I smashed on top of him, and Jamie fell flat on top of me.

"Well, this is a nice surprise," Mr. Humperdink said, turning down the volume on the *Castle* rerun on TV. It looked like both corners of his mouth were curling up, but since I wasn't used to seeing Mr. Humperdink smile, I figured it could have been gas.

"How're you doing, Mr. H?" asked Tom.

"Are we disturbing you?" I asked, as we scrambled up.

"Not at all, and much, much better, thank you," he answered.

"Guess I'd better be going," said a voice from the chair in the corner.

That voice.

Stefano Stefano.

Of Stefano Stefano's Ice Cream Parlor.

I nearly fainted on the spot.

"You kids all know Mr. Stefano, don't you?" Mr. Humper-dink asked.

Jamie nodded, her eyes wide, and kept nodding, really getting into that bobblehead thing.

"Have a seat," said the probable spy, drug kingpin, hired assassin—and recent purveyor of Mexican fine foods. He stood, turned to Jamie who was nearest him, and gallantly motioned to his chair.

"Nice to meet you." Tom shook hands with Stefano Stefano while I paled and pushed behind Jamie to sit in the chair. Jamie and I hadn't clued in Tom to our suspicions about the Stefanos, but a million thoughts spun around in my brain as I tried to figure out what Stefano Stefano was doing visiting Mr. Humperdink.

Whatever it was, it had to be bad.

"See you tomorrow—with peach pie and blueberry-peppermint crunch ice cream?" Stefano Stefano asked Mr. Humperdink, as he walked to the door.

"Sounds wonderful," Mr. Humperdink answered, waving good-bye.

"It sure does," I murmured under my breath.

"We just ate," Tom whispered.

"She's a bottomless pit," Jamie whispered back to Tom. "No one knows where it all goes."

"So, how did you rascals get past Nurse Iron Bars?" Mr. Humperdink asked, the corners of his mouth doing that curling up thing again as he turned to look at us.

"I told her I was your nephew, but she muttered something about smoke and gray ice and told us we couldn't fool her. I think she's a little off." Tom pointed his index finger at the side of his head and twirled.

I looked at Jamie, she looked at me, and we both had to bite our lips to keep from laughing. Tom definitely hadn't caught on yet about how famous those smoky gray Weaver eyes were in River Creek.

"We waited for her break, and snuck past," Tom continued. "How have you been feeling, Mr. H?"

"Much better today. Had an awful headache yesterday, but it's easing up a bit."

"When are they gonna let you kick this popsicle stand?" Tom asked.

"Nurse Iron Bars said tomorrow or the day after, if I behave and keep resting."

"Mr. H.," Tom hesitated for a moment, "I've been wondering. Did you see the guys who clobbered you?"

"I wish I had. I'll tell you one thing," and he looked straight at Tom as he said it, "I'd sure like to thank whoever called 911. My blood pressure went wacky from that conk. If the paramedics hadn't gotten me to the hospital as fast as they did..."

Tom looked down. I could see that he was trying not to go fuchsia-faced, but it was no use. One of these days I'm going to have to teach that kid my old thinking-of-the-evil-Brussels-sprouts-to-keep-from-blushing trick.

"Mr. Humperdink, did you see anything weird the night of the robbery?" I asked, trying to sound like I was just making conversation.

"Well, there were a few things that slipped under my radar." He paused to sip his cranberry juice. "I was a bit preoccupied, you see, when I went in Friday night, but I'm almost certain that after I walked inside, I wasn't sure whether I'd had to unlock the door."

"Were there any other things," Jamie asked, "you know, that slipped under your radar?"

"I couldn't swear to it, but I remember—at least I think I remember—seeing a delivery truck parked behind the store."

"What color was it?" I blurted, hopping up.

"Well, it looked black, but who knows. You see, yesterday in the hospital was a foggy blur, so I can't be sure if I saw that truck or dreamed it up later."

Mr. Humperdink caught my sideways glance at Jamie. He narrowed his eyes and wagged his finger at us. "You kids are up to something."

"We're just worried, Mr. H.," Tom answered.

"I still don't get why anyone would steal a chubby brown bear, a two-toothed cougar, a mangy-lookin' lion, and every single guppy," I said.

"Could be they had a buyer for the whole kit and caboodle," said Mr. Humperdink.

"Or maybe they were trying to trick the police," said Jamie.

Mr. Humperdink scratched his head and nodded. "You may be on to something there, young lady. But if that's what they were up to, I'm afraid they didn't fool anyone."

He paused, looking at each of us as he dropped his bombshell. "You see, Lily's no ordinary Queen of the Jungle. Fact is, she's a white lion, and anyone who knows beans about lions would never dye a white lion's fur. They are sublime creatures of uncommon beauty... extremely valuable... but in the wrong hands—"

"I thought I told you!" Nurse Iron Bars snapped, barging in. "No one under eighteen unless you're a relative. And you are not relatives!" She looked directly at Tom's eyes.

"It's okay," Mr. Humperdink assured her. "My young friends here are cheering me up."

"Tiring you out and bringing in all kinds of germs, more like. Did you children so much as wash your hands before you came into this room? Show me your fingernails!"

I crossed my arms, Tom shoved his hands into his pockets, and Jamie hid hers behind her back. Nurse Iron Bars plucked Tom's hands out of his pockets and grimaced. "If he's caught an infection because of you—"

"We'd better be going," said Jamie, as we rushed to the door.

"Hope we didn't disturb you," I said, then in a burst of bravado, turned back and asked, "By the way, I was just wondering, what was Mr. Stefano doing here?"

"He's an old friend. We..."

"Out, out, out!" Nurse Iron Bars swatted the air at us.

"Get well soon, Mr. H," Tom called.

As we got into the elevator and rode downstairs, I wondered whether Stefano Stefano had known about Lily all along. I'd bet my next double chocolate Oreo hot fudge sundae that he was just pretending to be Mr. Humperdink's friend to get information about Lily since he was obviously in cahoots with the bad guys. Heck, Stefano Stefano was probably the ringleader of the whole operation.

Poor Mr. Humperdink. I'd hate it if Jamie were just pretending to like me so I'd help her with math and let her hang out in Fort Bamboo. And as I thought about how lucky I was to have a best friend like Jamie, my heart warmed right up and melted away the last little bits of my angriness.

"It's getting late." The elevator doors opened and Tom walked into the lobby. "I have to go home."

"Now?" Jamie followed him.

"Oh no!" I exclaimed.

"We'll be your lookouts, just like yesterday," said Jamie.

"I forgot to give Mr. Humperdink the papaya."

Jamie pulled me out of the elevator. "You can't go back upstairs."

"I need to get home before dinner to check—" Tom began.

"Dinner! I'm supposed to be home for a family dinner." Jamie turned to Tom. "But how will you—"

"It's okay. Yesterday I figured out how to sneak from our neighbor's backyard to our hidden den window so Messy-red-headed guy and Brown-buzz guy can't spot me."

"Please give this to Mr. Humperdink in Room 454." I placed the papaya on the Security Guard's desk. He was a lot younger than the security guy who'd been there earlier. "It's a one-of-a-kind, rare, tropical, very important—"

The guard pulled out an earphone and scrunched his mouth over to the left side of his face. "What?"

"Papaya," I shouted. "Room 454."

I raced over to Tom and Jamie before he had a chance to say no.

Nineteen

"Ahhhhh—ohh—glu-unk!"

I gasped and gulped down my mouthful of Chocolate Monsoon Madness cake.

"You have got to stop sneaking up on us!" I scowled at Tom. He was standing smack in front of me at the entrance to Fort Bamboo, origami cranes dangling in his stringy blond hair.

"How...?" I began.

Tom pointed to the rope ladder.

I'd done it again. I turn eleven and—BOOM—I forget to pull up the rope ladder two nights in a row. This getting older stuff was looking tougher than I'd thought.

"Don't tell me—you guys just woke up." Tom smirked.

"Funny." I made a face, then reached under my bunk for the platter of leftover cake.

"Here." I handed it to Tom.

"Darn." Jamie frowned. "Bad timing."

Clutching the platter against his chest, Tom looked up at Jamie then back down at the cake. "Bad timing?"

"I wanted to see the pictures we took at Chan's on Indy's phone yesterday, but Mr. Bamboo rigs up their computers to do this self-repair thing every Tuesday morning."

Tom relaxed his death grip on the platter. "How about if we bring our clues to Mr. Wilson at his farm," he shoved a handful of cake in his mouth, "and look at the pictures later."

"Isn't this when you guys use sibling blackmail to get Cody and Elizabeth to drive us?" I asked.

"Yeah, but we have to find 'em first," Tom answered.

"And Elizabeth's not answering her phone," said Jamie, still holding my phone.

"Then let's get out of here!" I picked up my backpack, swung it over my shoulder, and swooped down the rope ladder with Jamie and Tom behind me.

We rode our bikes toward Main Street, crossing up every side street and down every alley along the way in case Cody and Elizabeth were locking lips beside a building somewhere. We had just passed Bartholomew Jackson's house and were edging up to the Loyal Order of the Loping Antelope Lodge when—

"Ah-choo!"

Someone was on our tail. I whipped my head around, nearly toppling over, and saw... no one?

"That's weird," I said.

"What's weird?" asked Jamie.

"Did you hear something?"

"Nope." Jamie shrugged.

"Never mind," I said, taking one more look around as I coasted up to Stefano Stefano's take-out window. "Anybody want ice cream?"

"Sure." Tom gave his stomach a hard pat. "It'll go with the cake."

I handed Jamie some money to order for me. "Blueberry-peppermint crunch on a sugar cone, okay? Be right back."

On my way to the restroom, for old times' sake, I peeked in the party room where Jamie and I'd had our birthday parties every year since forever, until we started having sleepover parties in Fort Bamboo instead. My eyes were drawn like magnets to the half-eaten High School Special on the table— ten scoops of chocolate cookie dough and double chocolate Oreo with mountains of Stefano Stefano's home made hot fudge, whipped cream, Marshmallow Fluff, and M&M's.

I stood there wishing I'd ordered double chocolate Oreo and didn't even notice the size twenty shoes poking out from underneath the table until a familiar gravelly voice rumbled from the other side of the booth. My heart pounded a hundred thousand miles a minute as I threw myself against the wall to listen.

"...eleven o'clock. Sharp," Brown-buzz guy snarled. "You be there with the money—all the money—or you're never gonna see that cuddly bear and his furry friends again—except warm and snuggly on someone else's back. Get my drift?"

A glint from the florescent ceiling light bounced off a shiny bald head. A chair leg scraped the linoleum floor.

I wasn't sure if Brown-buzz guy was just getting comfortable—or if he'd spotted me—and I sure as heck wasn't waiting to find out. I raced out of the store so fast, I knocked the cone out of Tom's hands and sent his two scoops of vanilla cookie dough flying.

"Hey!" Tom yelled.

I motioned for them to follow me. "Brown-buzz guy... inside. I think... not sure... might have seen me."

We hopped on our bikes, rode around to the next driveway, and parked behind Angel's Video Games.

"Where's the truck? The only car in Stefano's lot is Mr. and Mrs. Stefano's prehistoric Pontiac," Jamie said, oblivious to the ice cream dripping down her arm as she juggled our cones in one hand and held the handlebars with the other.

"Something big—real big—is happening tonight." I lowered my voice. "I heard Brown-buzz guy say that at 'eleven o'clock sharp,' the other guy better bring the money, or he was turning Lily and all the other animals into fur coats. I think he was talking to that Shiny-bald-headed guy—the one we saw him talking to at the Lodge."

"Oh... my... God." Jamie raised both eyebrows above eyes that were round with worry.

"It could be eleven in the morning, too," Tom suggested, "or another day, like... Friday?" But he didn't look even a tiny bit convinced as he said it.

"But if it's tonight, we only have the rest of today to find them." Jamie began twirling her ponytails.

"We have to warn Mr. Humperdink. I'll bet Stefano Stefano's the brains behind the whole heist," I said.

"Are you nuts?" Tom asked. Jamie and I still hadn't clued him in to our Mr. and Mrs. Stefano Stefano theories.

"It's his store, and they were meeting there, and Jamie and I have lots of reasons to—"

"The truck!" Tom shouted.

"Let's go!" I called.

We sped out of the parking lot, but by the time we started down Main Street, the truck had disappeared.

"We lost 'em." Tom jumped off his bike.

"Again," I said.

"Yuck!" Jamie wiped her left arm on her t-shirt. It was a mush of melted blueberry-peppermint crunch and double chocolate Oreo ice cream, the empty cones crunched to crumbs in her hand.

"Let's ride back to my house. The computers should be ready by now, and you can get cleaned—"

Duh Dun! Duh Dun!
Duh Dun Dun Dun Dun Dun!!!!!

"Stars and Stripes Forever" boomed from my pocket.

"Your phone!" Jamie covered her ears while I melted with mortification. How could Dad have used my secret—as in *secret*—favorite song for my ringtone? Next thing you know, he'll take out a front page ad in *The River Creek Gazette* that I still sleep with Wuzzy Bear.

"Hello?" Jamie grabbed the phone, then held her arm straight out so she wouldn't go deaf, as Mom, blasting even louder than the entire Marine Corps Band, shouted, "...Piano recital... An hour late... Grounded... Rehearsal... *Home this instant!*"

"I'm not going." I frowned when Jamie hung up.

"Did you not hear the word, 'grounded?'" said Jamie.

"It'll take all day," I said, climbing back on my bike. "If the meeting's tonight—"

"You won't be doing anything tonight, tomorrow, or for every miserable day of middle school if you don't go now!" Jamie raised her right eyebrow just the tiniest bit. "Or have you already forgotten the last time you were POM'd?"

Prisoner of Mom'd. How could I forget? For five friend-less, Fort Bamboo-less, chocolate-less days, I'd had to help Mom organize her sewing room, and if there's a word for the opposite of Feng Shui, her sewing room is it.

"All right, all right," I grumbled. "I'll go home to change my clothes, but I'm sneaking out of the rehearsal first chance I get, and you guys have to keep—"

"I'll find Cody," said Tom.

"I'll look for Elizabeth," said Jamie. "Come get me if you escape. Otherwise, I'll see you at your recital, and we can all meet tomorrow morning—at Joy-Lynn's?"

"Fine." I sighed.

If Mom and Miss DeBow didn't kill me first.

TWENTY

I was going straight to my rehearsal when my stomach started its Grrrrrr-umph-urgle-urgle-urgling. I squished it in, but that only made it Grrrrrr-umph-urgle louder, and wouldn't you know it? The Lucky's Burger Café pink and red striped awning popped up right out of nowhere.

I tried not to go in, but there was no way I'd survive without starving to death while Miss DeBow made us practice our pieces over and over again. I'd just as likely starve to death after my recital, too. Now that my birthday was over, it was back to the one food that's been making me question Mom's unconditional love—the evil Brussels sprouts, which she thinks I can't see, taste, or smell in my slime green oatmeal.

I parked my bike and went inside to order.

"Hey, Indy." Jamie's sister Martha Alice smiled and waved from a booth with a bunch of her friends. "You look nice."

"Th-anks." I waved back. I've known Martha Alice for my entire life, but whenever I see her around town with the other popular, going into the eighth grade girls at Martin Memorial Middle School, I morph into a tongue-tied goofball. Lucky for me, they're always too busy being popular to notice.

"What can I get you, Indiana?" Mrs. Lucky Pike called from the kitchen as I sat down at the counter.

"A large order of fries, to go, please."

"Sweet potato, skinny dippers, or curly?" she asked.

"Curly, extra-crispy," I said.

"Anything to drink?"

"A chocolate sha... Holy Guacamole!" I jumped back, then slowly bent down to peek out from the corner of the picture window. My brain couldn't believe what my eyes were seeing. Messy-red-headed guy was talking to some kid with stringy blond... it couldn't be...

"Guacamole? You know we only serve burgers, shakes, and—"

"Shhhhhh!" I shooed her away as she walked to the counter.

Uh. Oh.

There was icy silence as every molecule in the room froze in mid-air. Icy, grown-up silence. I turned to face Mrs. Lucky Pike, whose smile had flipped upside down and whose blue eyes had just shrunk so small they could fit inside a ladybug's spot.

Mrs. Lucky Pike almost never has a temper. But when she does...

"Sorry... I'm hiding... I mean playing... um... hide and seek, and I was thinking... well, I wasn't exactly thinking, but..."

The air unfroze and the molecules began colliding happily around the room as her mouth flipped back into a smile. "I used to have so much fun playing hide and seek with Emily when she was little..."

While she reminisced about little Emily, who's been married and living in Indianapolis ever since the Great Lucky's Burger Café non-robbery, I angled my body so I could take another peek.

There was no sign of Tom, but Messy-red-headed guy was still outside, talking on his phone. He looked up and walked toward us.

"Bathroom!" I interrupted Mrs. Lucky Pike, with an apologetic shrug.

I raced in and locked the door, then smushed my ear against it to listen while Messy-red-headed guy ordered four Jumbo Burger and Fry Specials.

I couldn't breathe. Or blink.

I turned the knob slowly and opened the door a sliver.

Messy-red-headed guy was sitting at the counter.

In Public.

I glanced at Martha Alice and her friends, then remembered that no one else—besides Jamie, Tom, and me—knows that he's a head-conking, puppy-purloining, Maurice the Bear-stealing, bad guy.

Mrs. Lucky Pike bagged his order. She went to the register to ring him up. He started walking to the door but stopped to look at his cell phone. Then she put my fries and shake in a bag, plopped in the ketchup and salt packets, and walked back to the register.

My heart was thumping so loud its echo boomeranged from my ribs to the bathroom walls and back again.

Don't call my name. Please! Don't call my...

He was gone.

With one jerky breath, relief flooded every single cell of my body.

For half a second.

At most.

What the heck was Tom doing talking to Messy-red-headed guy? I tried to think of one single good reason. Oh, there was a reason, all right, but it was a no-good rotten one. Tom was in on it, just like I'd thought at the start. But why was he hanging around pretending to be friends with us? Maybe...

"Burgersandfries... burgersandfries... burgersandfries!" The Lucky's cuckoo bird blared from the pink polka dot clock just as my phone blasted "Stars and Stripes Forever."

"Almost there!" I called into my phone. Grabbing my bag, I inhaled a fistful of fries and half my chocolate shake then hopped on my bike before Mom could say the "G" word again.

I tiptoed into the common room of the First Presbyterian Church and slid into the last row while Ollie Eaton played "The March of the Tin Soldiers," but Miss DeBow spotted me, and pointed to the empty seat next to Autumn in the front.

I tried not to fidget on my cold, hard, metal folding chair, but I swear Miss DeBow has special powers to make time crawl.

When it was finally my turn, she stopped me after nine measures and said as impressive as it was that I could make "The Waltz of the Flowers" sound surprisingly like "The Flight of the Bumblebee," I needed to slow down and express "emotion, emotion, emotion!"

After five more tries, Miss DeBow looked straight up as if only Heaven could help us now, then ordered me back to my seat to pay special attention as Autumn played "Night on Bald Mountain" with such "lovely, deep feeling." Autumn looked to me like the only thing she was feeling deeply about was turning herself into an Auntie Anne's jumbo pretzel as she bent every which way over the piano.

By the time I was back at the piano twisting myself into enough of a double pretzel of my own to satisfy Miss DeBow, it was too late to escape. My parents were walking in. It was time for the recital.

Jamie and her mom would be here any minute. I couldn't wait to hear if Jamie had any luck prying Elizabeth and Cody out of fishface mode so she could ask them to drive us to Mr. Wilson's farm.

If Jamie ever got here.

Which she didn't.

After the recital, I called and called, but there was no answer. When we drove by her house on the way home, it was dark.

I went to bed and kept falling asleep—almost—but just as everything got all nice and dreamy—

Ahhhhhhhhhh! Tom's smoky gray eyes peered down at me just like they did when he woke us up in Fort Bamboo... and then I started worrying all over again about the meeting, and what if it was tonight, and the animals were gone forever, and—

I bolted straight up in bed.

What if... somehow...

I had to get to Joy-Lynn's in the morning before Tom did.

I had to warn Jamie about Tom.

Twenty-one

"Boo!"

"Tom!" I jumped, dropping my bike in front of the bike rack.

"That bad, huh?"

"What?"

He scratched that stringy blond hair. "Your piano recital..."

I stared at him while we walked up to Joy-Lynn's.

"Any luck with Cody?" Jamie asked, as she walked out of Joy-Lynn's with three giant cookies.

"Nope. How about Elizabeth?"

Jamie shook her head. "No time alone to ask."

"Where were you?" I squeaked in an unnaturally high voice.

Tom looked at me, wrinkling his mouth.

He knows, I thought. He knows that I know.

"Indy, I'm sorry," said Jamie. "I left you a message. Elizabeth's soccer team won, so we had to go to Bloomington for the semi-finals."

Tom was still staring at me. "Don't you want your cookie?"

Under ordinary circumstances, the fact that I'd just finished the last slice of Chocolate Monsoon Madness Cake for breakfast would never get in the way of a giant Joy-Lynn's chocolate chip cookie, but nerves had filled up the empty spaces in my tummy where the cookie was supposed to go.

"Are you okay?" Jamie asked. I guess the meaningful looks I kept trying to give her looked more goofy than meaningful. Why, why, why hadn't we invented a secret code, like, "How's the weather in Madagascar?" for Bad Guy Emergencies?

"You traitor!" I blurted.

"I'm... sorry?" said Jamie, her eyes clouding over.

"You sneaky, lying, Paradise Pet robbing... robber!" I continued.

Jamie stared at me like I'd lost it. Tom went pale. He glanced at Jamie with a "Does she crack up this way often?" look, but I wasn't falling for his Mr. Innocent Act for another millisecond.

"He's in on it—Paradise Pets! I saw him talking to Messy-red-headed guy yesterday outside Lucky's!"

"Are you out of your mind?" Tom said.

"Tom... with... Messy?" Jamie asked at the same time.

"I saw him... his hair, his clothes—"

"I haven't been anywhere near Lucky's!" Tom's voice rose.

"How can you be sure it was—" Jamie began.

"Prove it!" I demanded.

"I don't have to prove anything!" Tom turned to leave, his oatmeal cookie crumbling as his hands squeezed into fists.

Jamie's face turned pink and puffy, then puffier and puffier until she was about to erupt, in tears or anger, or just plain confusion. She started to twirl her ponytails, so I grabbed her arm before she could go into total Jamie bounce mode.

"Let's get out of here," I said. "We don't have time for traitors."

But as we rode our bikes to my house, a wave of miserableness washed over me.

Tom Weaver was in cahoots with the bad guys.

Which made him Stringy-blond guy.

And definitely not our friend.

Maybe all the Weavers were bad news, smoky gray eyes and all, not that I'd especially noticed or—

"Jamie," I cried and swerved behind a maple tree. "Get back!"

"Why?" Jamie leapt off her bike.

"What's Stefano Stefano doing going into the Lodge?"

"Having a late lunch?" Jamie shrugged. She didn't trust him any more than I did, but I had to admit it was a possibility.

We wheeled closer and saw a bunch of cars in the back parking lot.

"What's going on?" I asked.

We dropped our bikes behind the shrubs lining the driveway, and Jamie inched ahead.

"This way." She motioned for me to follow as she slipped in through a side door.

Looking around the Lodge's dark, moldy basement, I whispered, "As long as we're here...," but I didn't have to say more.

We started searching for clues, or maybe... just maybe... some of the animals, though this place didn't look, smell or sound like any living creature—with the possible exception of the furnace repair man, a gang of slippery, slimy beetles, or an occasional mouse—had been here in this lifetime or the last.

We'd already searched the furnace room and the empty storage area when I climbed up a half-staircase into the most beautiful room I'd ever seen. It had tall, white Indiana limestone columns on each side of a small stage, and fancy wood paneling on the walls.

The coolest part of all was the domed ceiling, just like the stained glass dome at the Indiana State Capitol, except this dome had an antelope-shaped skylight in the middle. The sunbeam shining through it made that antelope leap clear across the floor.

"Hello," boomed a voice from outside the entrance to the auditorium.

"How's it going?" boomed another. "Long time, no see."

Jamie hurried up the stairs to see what was going on.

Men in suits, men in overalls, men with giant red flowers on Hawaiian shirts, and Mrs. Evie Evermore filed into the auditorium.

We ducked back into the stairwell and eased the door closed, leaving it just a crack open.

"How could I have forgotten?" Jamie moaned and slapped her forehead. "June 21st! The Summer Solstice!"

I wasn't happy as a clam to be inside, either, on the longest, best outside day of the whole year, but I sure wouldn't have expected Jamie to take it so hard.

"What—" I began, but was interrupted by Ernie Evermore, the sole proprietor of the Evermore Funeral Home.

He stood alone on the stage wearing puke-brown, plastic antlers, and his trademark yellow overalls with the slogan, "EVERMORE FOR THE EVERAFTER," sewn in huge orange letters across—and there's no polite way to say this—his unnaturally wide behind—a behind which you can be sure has never done the bicycle at Joy-Lynn's Bakery, Exercise Emporium, and Special Occasion Beauty Salon.

Ernie looked into the audience, and with a solemn expression, he reached behind his impossible to look at, but impossible to ignore, behind and pulled out a caramel-colored kitten, which he held up with his left hand while it wriggled and squirmed.

I wondered where he'd been hiding it for all that time, and the picture that popped into my brain of the poor kitty squished into a back pocket of Ernie's overalls wasn't pretty. Then, just as fast, that picture flew out of my brain because Ernie reached down to the floor behind the podium and pulled out a silver sword.

"Oh, Great Antelope in the sky," he bellowed, swinging the sword in circles above his head.

My heart flopped as he barked, "Eeerk, Eeerk," sounding like a dog imitating a seal imitating a dog. He waved his hands to urge the other men and Mrs. Evie Evermore to Eeerk along with him.

"We offer thanks for your munificence. Eeerk, Eeerk," he barked again, and a bunch of the men, in particular, the puke-brown-plastic-antler-wearing ones, joined in.

"And offer you this gift."

I tried to close my eyes, but my eyelids were stuck. Then I tried to cover my eyes, but my hands wouldn't move. I was pretty sure I was going to be sick when Ernie raised his sword and sliced through the air.

Men Eeerked.

I gasped.

Jamie laughed. "Indy, open your eyes."

I guess somehow, in the middle of all that Eeerking, my eyelids unstuck themselves from being stuck open because now they were stuck shut.

"C'mon, Indy. You know Ernie Evermore wouldn't hurt a flea. He's a joker…" Jamie went on and on, until I squinted my right eye open just a peek, and sure enough, Ernie Evermore stood on the stage with the kitten cuddled in his arms. He touched her head softly with the sword and placed a tiny pink crown between her ears.

"Gentle feline," he said, as she wriggled and squirmed and shook the crown off, "we anoint you Summer Solstice, Queen of the Light."

The men and Evie Evermore laughed and Eeerked and stomped their feet so hard the floor vibrated all the way up to my ears.

Ernie motioned for everyone to calm down. "We have a special guest joining us all the way from his ranch in Texas. He's the great-great grandson of Otto Flavours, the First, LOLA's beloved founder and the founder of Fabulous Flavours. Put your hands together and give a big LOLA welcome to our guest of honor, Otto Flavours, the Fourth."

While they all clapped and Eeerked, something round and shiny as a crystal ball bounced toward the stage. Ernie stepped back, and it felt like a backhoe had just dug a pit in my stomach.

The round and shiny something was a head—Shiny-bald-headed guy's head, to be precise, and I swear, that guy must have polished it up with Pledge to get it to shine like that.

He was standing at the podium talking, but I wasn't hearing. The pit in the place my stomach used to be got bigger and bigger as I realized this giant, Shiny-bald-headed guy towering over Ernie Evermore was the same Shiny-bald-headed guy who'd looked practically Munchkin-like next to Brown-buzz guy at the Lodge on Sunday.

He must have finished talking because all of a sudden, everyone was standing up, walking out to the front hall, and clomping up the stairs to eat.

Jamie started tiptoeing back to the basement. I didn't move.

"Indiana, c'mon!"

I raised my right hand, curled my fingers slowly, and pointed to the stage. "That guy..."

"Bald as a baby's behind. I know," she said, "but I don't want my dad..."

"Holy Guacamole! That's your dad!" I said to Jamie, as it registered that he was one of the non-puke-brown-antler-wearing LOLA guys standing up in the first row. I'd been looking straight past him for the entire time that I'd been staring at Shiny-bald-headed guy on the stage.

"...to see us here," Jamie continued, tugging my arm.

When Otto Flavours, the First, founded LOLA, he made a rule that every adult who'd ever lived in River Creek was automatically a member forever unless he or she quit three times. The story is on a plaque outside about how some snooty old club in Chicago snubbed Otto big time before he got rich.

Once he got rich and became THE Otto Flavours of Fabulous Flavours Pet Products, that snooty old club tried and tried to get him to join, but he said no-thank-you-very-much, except he didn't say it that politely. Then he turned around and started the Loyal Order of the Loping Antelope Lodge.

My parents are still members, far as I know, but I figure they're too absent-minded to remember to go to the meetings. I hope old Otto Flavours, the First, if he's looking down on River Creek, won't think I'm being rude and ungrateful, but when I grow up, I'm going to be sure to forget to go to those meetings, too.

In fact, after what I saw today, I am never going to another meeting of the Loyal Order of the Loping Antelope again in my whole entire life.

Ever.

In a million years.

"Indiana!"

Jamie grabbed my arm, and we were out of there in a flash.

Twenty-two

We were rushing to our bikes behind the shrubs when Jamie stopped in her tracks.

"Otto Flavours, the Fourth, is...?" She pointed to the Lodge.

"Shiny-bald-headed guy." I straddled my bike and motioned for her to get moving.

"What the heck is a rich guy like Otto Flavours, the Fourth, doing in cahoots with Messy-red-headed and Brown-buzz guys?"

"All those animal heads in the Lodge. Maybe he wants more. Maybe things aren't as different nowadays as we thought," I said, as we rode down Seventeenth Street toward my driveway.

"Ah-choo!"

"Did you hear that?" I stopped short and jerked my head around to see who'd sneezed.

"What?" Jamie asked.

Jamie looked to the left. I looked to the right. We both looked behind us.

No one.

"I think Ernie Evermore really got to you with his kitten routine," said Jamie, as we got going again.

"I could have sworn I heard—"

hhhmmmmmmMMMMMMMMMMMMMMMM!!!

The low hum behind us grew louder. And louder. Rubber burned, tires squealed, and Jamie yelped. Brown-buzz guy wrenched the steering wheel as the truck veered off to the left while Messy-red-headed guy glowered at me with a crooked, crisscross, evil jack-o-lantern smile.

"Are you okay?" I jumped off my bike. "Jamie!"

Jamie was on the ground, her bike down on top of her leg. I lifted her bike. She took off her helmet, ran her fingers through her sweat-soaked hair, and folded up like an accordion.

"Messy-red... Buzz... tried to kill me." Her voice was so quiet I had to lean close to her to hear. "They... aimed truck... right at me... tried to..."

"Nah." I shook my head extra hard to convince myself, too. "They're just trying to scare us."

"They're coming back!" Jamie cried. I'd never seen her look so terrified.

The truck slowed as it neared us. The passenger door opened. I looked around to see if anyone was outside, but Seventeenth Street was not what you'd call hopping.

"Your leg?" I helped her up.

Jamie shook her head. "It's okay."

We got back on our bikes. The door of the truck slammed shut, and the engine V-roomed.

"Follow me!" Tom appeared out of nowhere, speeding by—on my dad's bike, no less.

"No way!" I stopped riding, but Jamie was already halfway down the street behind him.

The engine roared as the truck got closer.

I raced to catch up as Tom sped under Mrs. Granger's grape arbor, across Sixteenth Street, and through three backyards until we came out again on Seventeenth and Redbud, right in front of my house.

Tom threw down his bike and collapsed on our lawn. "We lost 'em."

Jamie collapsed next to Tom. I collapsed next to Jamie, resting my head on my hands.

Then I felt it. The ground began to vibrate, the road began a slow rumble, and that low hum growled in the distance. Creeping down Seventeenth Street, its bug-eyed headlights swinging from side to side, the black truck loomed, coming closer by the second.

"We didn't lose 'em." I glared at Tom, a lump about the size of a grapefruit in my throat. "You led them to my front door."

TWENTY-THREE

"You're out of your…," Tom began, but he was drowned out as the engine V-roomed, then sputtered, as the truck slowed to a crawl in front of us.

"Let's go." Tom climbed on his bike.

"Jamie! No!" I yelled. Before I could stop her, Jamie was riding behind Tom again, and I sure as heck wasn't letting her follow him alone.

Tom raced down Redbud, ditched his bike behind the tool shed in Mr. Gerardo's backyard, and did a dead man's fall flat on the ground. Then he rolled straight into a patch of milkweed until he hit a small, wooden cellar door that appeared out of nowhere.

"Down here." He opened the narrow door.

"Not a chance!" I didn't move. Tom was leading us right into a trap.

Brakes squealed. A door slammed.

Thud. SMACK. Thud. SMACK. Thud. SMACK.

Someone big was thumping toward us. Someone very big.

I dropped my bike and leapt inside, if you'd call squeezing myself through the cellar door like a stuffed sausage leaping.

"Jamie, hurry!" Tom called.

She had stopped cold.

A gimongous black spider, its body the size of a Double Stuf Oreo cookie and each of its eight legs the size of a furry caterpillar, balanced like a bushy bullseye on its giant web in the middle of the doorway. I shuddered, feeling creepy-crawlies all over me, then shook out my hair and brushed and brushed and brushed myself off.

"Black widow," Jamie croaked.

"Wolf spider." Tom swatted it off the web.

Jamie screamed. I grabbed her shirt and dragged her into the black hole under the cellar door. Tom closed the door on top of us.

Darkness. Total complete darkness. There was no light at all, not even one skinny ray slipping through a crack in the doors. Jamie squeezed my hand until my bones crunched, but the truth of it was that scared as she was of spiders, I was about as scared to be cramped in a tiny, dark place with barely enough oxygen for even that wolf spider to breathe.

"Follow me." Tom pulled Jamie behind him.

"We're not moving a muscle until you tell us where we're going, Tom Weaver." I jerked Jamie back toward me.

"It's a tunnel, and it leads straight to… well, you'll see in a few minutes if I don't miss our turn," Tom answered.

"Miss our turn!" Just what I wanted to hear. "And you expect us to follow you to your evil trap through this dark, oxygenless—"

"You wanna get run over by Brown-buzz and Messy-red-headed guys, fine by me. Let's go, Jamie," said Tom.

Jamie jolted forward as Tom pulled her away from me. I pulled her back again, hard as I could.

"Cut it out!" Jamie shook us off. "What do you two think I am, your personal wishbone?"

"How do we know it's not a trap?" I said.

"What choice do we have?" said Jamie. "Besides, that stringy-blond-haired boy you saw could have been half the boys in River Creek, not to mention Cody or any of Tom's brothers."

"It was T—" I began.

"C'mon." Jamie yanked my arm.

Thwack!

"Ow!" I winced as my elbow smacked the wall.

I looked ahead into the dark nothingness, and my body froze. My stomach ached with terror.

"Sorry," Jamie yanked my still tingling arm harder, "but I'm not going without you."

We walked in silence, feeling our way along the damp earth wall. I kept trying to hold off my claustrophobic panic, but it wasn't working. My eyes watered. I could hardly breathe. When I finally managed to take a breath, the air smelled so much like dirt, I could taste it right through my nostrils.

"Duck!" Tom said. The tunnel ceiling dipped down, and we dropped to our hands and knees.

"Ow!" I winced again, as my right knee hit the ground. It was still smarting from being torn up at the Lodge.

A scratchy pitterpat distracted me from my pain. "What's that?"

Tiny little feet landed on my head, skittered across my back, and leapt off. Goosebumps jumped from my arms. My insides jiggled like cranberry jelly.

"Rats! Get them off me! Get them off!" I hollered.

"Rats…" Jamie's voice evaporated into a thin whisper.

"Those aren't rats. There aren't any rats down here," Tom said. "Just keep going."

"Like we have a choice," I answered. So I'm afraid of rats. Who knew. The only rat I happen to be on a first-name basis with practically purrs whenever I pet her, but Fat Cat, my Aunt Wilma's science lab rescue rat, isn't your average disease-carrying, pointy-toothed rodent.

Tom stopped crawling. I reached through the air and felt a wall in front of us. We'd hit a dead end.

My head was spinning. I wasn't sure how much more of this I could take.

"What now?" I demanded.

"We're here."

Tom pushed on the wall, a door flew open, and he flew through it.

I toppled on top of Jamie, and Jamie toppled on top of Tom, into a tiny, dark, airless cubby of a room.

"Where are we?" Jamie scrambled up.

Tom pushed on the opposite wall. A small door opened to another little room. He crouched low and walked out.

And then I knew. Brown-buzz and Messy-red-headed guys were waiting on the other side of that door to conk us just like they'd conked Mr. Humperdink. Tom had led us right into...

My living room? Underneath *my* Staircase to Nowhere from *my* half-room beneath the stairs.

A tidal wave of anger whooshed from my toes all the way up to the roots of my brown braids.

"How long have you been sneaking into our house?" I exploded.

"I just saved you from the bad guys!" Tom shouted even louder. "Did you forget that already?"

"Saved us? Ha!" I shouted so loud it hurt my throat. "How... long... have... you... been... sneaking... into... my... house?" I asked through gritted teeth.

"I've never snuck into your stupid house," he answered, his voice icy cold.

My cheeks burned with anger. "Oh yeah? Then I guess it really was a ghost we found hiding in the attic on Sunday."

His fists tight against his legs, he stormed to the front door. "Who needs you anyway? I'm out of here."

"Stop!" Jamie shouted loudest of all, shocking us both into silence.

"You," she raised her right eyebrow at Tom, "have got to stop threatening to leave every time you get your feelings hurt, and you," she raised her left eyebrow at me, "are apologizing for saying he was in cahoots with the bad guys."

Neither of us moved.

Well, maybe I kind of half-shrugged, but I was still half-expecting Brown-buzz and Messy-red-headed guys to turn up and conk us. You can't just do the hokey pokey, turn yourself around, and trust someone like he was your best friend since birth once you've untrusted him for what seemed like a real good reason.

"Tom," Jamie sighed, her hands on her hips, "how long have you known about that tunnel? Stop sulking and answer me."

"Cody showed me it once." Tom crossed his arms against his chest and pressed his lips into a line so pencil-thin they disappeared.

"When else?" she commanded with both her evil eyebrows.

"No 'else,'" Tom answered. "Cody used it that time to sneak in to meet Elizabeth when she was babysitting you," he glowered at me, "but I didn't actually follow him all the way into your house."

"You mean to tell me that you dragged us through that rat-infested, oxygenless tunnel without even knowing for sure where it was going?" My temples pulsed with my whooshing anger.

"We got here, didn't we?" He glared.

My stomach felt queasy, and I plopped on the floor. "If you've never been all the way through that tunnel before, how do you know those weren't rats running across our backs?"

Right on cue, a furry brown critter leapt out of Tom's pocket and skittered across the floor. Jamie shivered. I did a full body shudder. Peek-a-Boo emerged from out of nowhere and chased the critter until it disappeared inside the living room wall.

"See," Tom said. "A mouse."

"Great." I flopped my head into my hands. "Now an innocent field mouse is trapped forever in the wall of death, too."

"What?" Tom began. "It's not trapped. Field mice slip in and out..."

Images flitted across my brain of poor P.J., her little guinea pig body wasting away to skin and bones in the wall of death. "Jamie, we have to search for—"

"Indiana!" Jamie interrupted, bouncing up and down, "I just realized... do you know what just happened?"

"You mean that we could have been starved to death AND suffocated AND stuck in that tunnel forever?" Not to mention conked, I thought.

"I mean that tunnel and the tiny room next to the half-room under the Staircase to Nowhere."

As soon as Jamie said it, I knew. "The Underground Railroad." I turned and stared at Tom.

Jamie threw her arms around his neck, then backed away so fast neither of them had a chance to go fuchsia-faced. "But we've been looking for the Underground Railroad tunnels in this house for our whole lives," she said. "Why didn't we ever see those doors?"

"Because you have to be inside the tunnel. You can't see them from inside your house. Or open them, either," Tom said.

I switched my stare from Tom to the wall beneath the stairs.

"Hey, guys," said Jamie, "the pictures..."

"...from Chan's! Holy Guacamole—we almost forgot!" I rushed to the windows as Jamie reached for my phone and raced to the family room. There was no sign of the truck—or the bad guys, but I closed the drapes anyhow.

We didn't say a word as the pictures filled the computer screen. Then we all started talking at once.

"I can't read the license plate."

"Make it bigger."

"I don't see anything... wait—"

"What's that?"

"There!" I pointed to the lower left corner of the screen.

"A gold diamond. It's peeking through—near the bumper, just like—"

"The Fabulous Flavours Pet Products diamond."

"What's a pet food company doing stealing pets?"

"Maybe someone stole the truck and painted it black."

"Maybe it's someone who works at the company."

"How do we know the company isn't in on it?"

Tom looked stunned.

"Wait a minute."

We stopped talking.

He was twisting his left earlobe and going paler by the second.

"That must be how Messy-red-headed guy knew me, but didn't know me. Hank—my oldest brother—he's been working at Fabulous Flavours since spring break. I should have thought of it before."

"How could you have known?" Jamie asked. "Until we saw the gold diamond in the picture, we didn't know where the truck came from."

"And we still don't know if it was stolen," I said.

"We only know we're running out of time—if we're not too late, already. That meeting could be at eleven tonight," Tom said.

Jamie and Tom looked as miserable as I felt.

"We have to think." I pressed my hands against my head to squeeze everything we knew out of my brain.

"We need to warn Mr. Humperdink about Stefano Stefano," I finally said.

Jamie shook her head. "Isn't it pointless when we should—"

"We should go to the Lodge to look for more clues," Tom interrupted.

"Jamie and I already…"

"We should go to Mr. Wilson's to have the bowls analyzed," Jamie continued, "because—"

"That could take days!" I said. "We have to find out when and where that meeting is, and fast."

"Yeah—we can figure out how they got the animals out of Mr. H.'s store later," said Tom.

"I've got it!" I said. "Let's get cleaned up. We're going to Fabulous Flavours."

"But...," Jamie began.

"Look," I paced back and forth, "if we ask around at Fabulous Flavours, we'll find out who that Messy-red-headed guy is. I'm sure of it."

Jamie looked thoughtful. "But wouldn't the police know if a truck had been stolen from Fabulous Flavours?"

"Not if the guy who stole it is supposed to be making a delivery somewhere far away. But if we find out that Messy-red-headed guy has gone missing..."

"That would definitely be the kind of clue the police are looking for." I finished Tom's thought. "Then we—"

"Then we go to the police." Jamie lifted her right eyebrow in a definite don't-even-think-of-crossing-me way. "Deal?"

Tom held out his hand. "Deal," and they shook on it.

"Deal." I agreed and walked into the kitchen to nuke the last of the tortillas and beans left over from my birthday.

"Nourishment." I handed plates to Jamie and Tom. "We'll need it."

Twenty-four

"Elizabeth's still not answering." Jamie gave my phone back to me. "What's the use of having a cell phone if you never answer it?"

"So much for sibling blackmail," I said. "We'll have to ride bikes."

"Bikes?" Jamie started to bounce. "Down Labrador Lane?"

"Sure," said Tom.

But I could tell he wasn't happy about it. As we hurried to get our bikes from Mr. Gerardo's backyard, I wasn't exactly jumping for joy, either.

The thing is, nobody lives on Labrador Lane. Nobody ever has, far as I know. As we rode and rode, the trees and grass morphed into vacant lots with heaps of trash. It looked like some hidden pocket of town that just never was settled, and I couldn't help wondering why.

Until we eased around the bend to the Kibble Cut-Off.

The Fabulous Flavours factory rose before our eyes, a mutant monster version of my dad's bowling shirt, its yellow and black checks pulsing and bobbing across every square centimeter of the kibble castle's turrets and towers.

"Eeeewwwww!"

Jamie gagged. Tom coughed. I covered my nose and mouth.

We'd ridden into a smokestack burp, and when the Fabulous Flavours factory's smokestack burps, you don't want to be downwind.

We skidded across the gravel parking lot next to the long, low warehouse, a cloud of dirt on our heels.

"Ah-choo!"

"Did you hear that?" I stopped short, looking back toward Labrador Lane.

"What?" asked Tom.

"I thought I saw... I could have sworn I heard someone sneeze."

But there was no one in sight.

"It's the Labrador Lane creeps." Jamie glanced at the empty parking lot.

We walked up to the front entrance of the factory.

Tom opened the glass doors, but he didn't go inside. "No one in the lobby."

"Who wants to go first?" I said.

"What if someone comes?" Jamie asked. She looked like she was regretting this excursion more and more by the second.

"That's the idea, isn't it?" I peered past Tom at the black and yellow checked linoleum floor.

"We'll say our summer project is to research the Fabulous Flavours Corporation," said Tom.

"And since their very popular King's Kibble dog food is made in River Creek, our own hometown," I began, "we came to..."

"...see if we could visit their mascot, Rex," Tom finished.

Jamie's right eyebrow inched up.

"Don't give me that 'you are developing frightening criminal tendencies' evil eyebrow, Miss Sibling Blackmailer," I said, before she could say another word. "Besides, we can write about Rex and the kibble when school—"

"May I help you?" a musical voice interrupted before Jamie could do any more eyebrow raising.

We all turned at once to face River Creek's music teacher, covered from hat to shoes in black and yellow checks.

"Mrs. Delatroix?" we blurted in unison.

"Jamie, Indiana, Tom, what are you kids doing way out here on this lovely afternoon?"

"What are you doing here?" I sputtered.

She laughed. "I'm working here Sundays, Mondays, and Wednesdays this summer as a security guard. It's a pretty good gig. I get to wear this cool uniform," she swept her hands across her shoulders, "I get paid double on weekends, and I have plenty of time to play drums with my band."

There wasn't much chance of mistaking Mrs. Delatroix for a fashionista in that checkerboard get-up, but the rest sounded great. If I become a music teacher when I grow up, I want to be just like her. For our graduation from elementary school in May, she made up hysterical words to Beethoven's Fifth Symphony. Before long, you couldn't set foot from the Lionel Library to Lucky's Burger Café without hearing a River Creek fifth grader "da da da dumming" all over town.

"So?" she asked.

"We're having a scavenger hunt." The words popped out of my mouth.

"Do you know if a big," Tom held out his arms, "really big, tall guy with messy red hair works here, Mrs. Delatroix?"

"Sure do. There's a big guy with red hair who's been around lately. I think he's a long-haul driver."

"Do you know his name?"

"Sorry," she shook her head, "but even if I knew his name, I'm afraid I couldn't tell you, not even three of my favorite students. Company policy."

"Is he making deliveries now?" I asked.

"The plant is closed this week for summer vacation, but I think I saw him pulling out on Thursday. Can't stop the deliveries, vacation or no vacation."

"Was he, by any chance, driving with a really, really big guy with a brown buzz?" asked Jamie.

Mrs. Delatroix shrugged. "Not sure I'd have noticed. There's only one red-headed guy, so he kind of stands out. What's all this got to do with your scavenger hunt?"

"It's not a regular kind of scavenger hunt. It's more like, we spot people in town and try to guess where they work," Jamie answered.

"Well, we'd better get going." I pushed in front of Jamie so Mrs. Delatroix wouldn't catch the Tom-like fuchsia blush covering her face from cheekbone to cheekbone. "Thanks for your help, Mrs. Delatroix."

"Yeah, thanks," Tom and Jamie chorused in unison.

"See you in September. Ride carefully, now." She touched her head to remind us to wear our helmets.

We rode back around the bend and over to the curb to talk.

"He works here," I said.

"And he's on the road, which means he has a Fabulous Flavours truck," Tom added.

"Which he could have easily painted," said Jamie.

"But we still don't know if he stole it," I looked at Jamie, "and we're still not any closer to finding him or the animals."

"Maybe not, but we know more than we did before. Time is running out. We have to tell the police everything, about the food, the truck, what Tom saw the night the pet store was robbed, what you heard at Stefano's, Indy. Everything!" Jamie straddled her bike with her arms folded in front of her.

"And if they don't believe us?" Tom asked.

"We'll have to make them believe us," Jamie said.

"Let's ride back to town. Then we can decide," I said.

I needed time to think, but I didn't like the images hovering at the edge of my brain, and I wasn't having much luck pushing them away. My nightmare of Maurice all skinny and scrawny in his cage, and of Princess Penelope, whimpering and scared, played over and over like a bad rerun. If we were going to find them, it had better be soon, before they ended up in Timbuktu or Terre Haute—or worse.

Twenty-Five

We flew down Labrador Lane, raced across Main Street, and were zipping down Seventeenth Street when,

Glopglop Ratatatratatatratatatratatatsqueakkkkkkkkkkk

A clattering cacophony echoed from the sky. A flying jack-hammer twisted up inside a rainbow-colored balloon was dive-bombing right at us.

"What the heck?"

Jamie and I ducked for cover. Tom broke into a cheek-cracking smile and leapt off his bike. Flapping his legs and clapping his hands over his head, Tom looked like a dancing scarecrow as he whistled, cooed, and called, "Here boy, down here. C'mon, Hendrix."

The squawking mess of red, blue, and yellow feathers dove so close he grazed our hair. Tom reached up and grabbed him. "Hendrix! You're back!"

I'd never seen a boy so happy to see a bird and vice-versa. Hendrix nuzzled Tom's neck with his black and ivory beak. Tom hugged Hendrix so hard I thought he'd suffocate for sure. Then Hendrix escaped, flapping his wings and squawking something awful as Tom jumped up and down, trying to grab him again.

"He's trying to tell us something," I said. Hendrix is one beautiful bird, but he can't squawk on key to save his life.

"We'll never know what if we don't calm him down. When Hendrix gets worked up, there's no understanding a word he says," Tom replied, as Hendrix flew back into his arms.

"You've got to be kidding," said Jamie. "When birds talk, it doesn't mean anything. They just imitate the sounds they hear."

The fuchsia blush crept up Tom's neck. "There's just one way, but he won't like it if you're looking. You guys better wait," he looked around and pointed to nowhere in particular, "over there."

"Hold on. I have something he'll like." I pulled a melted Reese's Peanut Butter Cup from my pocket. "You're gonna love this, buddy."

"Indiana!" Tom shoved my arm just as Hendrix dipped his beak down to take it. "You could've killed him. Scarlet Macaws can't eat chocolate."

"Ooops. Sorry, Hendrix." I shrugged sheepishly and started walking. "How about if we just sit down here," I called over my shoulder as we plunked on the ground behind a giant red maple tree, "out of sight."

But we sneaked a peek, and when we did, it was worth it.

Tom Weaver had Hendrix cradled in his arms like a newborn baby. He was stroking Hendrix's red feathered head and singing "Blowin' in the Wind," his voice sweeter than sugar on honey.

"There's more to that boy than smoky gray eyes and a stovepipe hat," said Jamie.

"He's one surprising Weaver," I admitted. Not that I was exactly a Weaver expert.

"Hey!" Tom spotted us before we could pull our heads back behind the tree. "Well—I guess it's okay. Dylan always does the trick. Mr. H. sings it to him all the time. He says Hendrix is just an old hippie at heart."

But in half a heartbeat, Hendrix was talking and flapping like crazy.

"Squealratatatratat. I hear the train coming. Squawk.

"Straight ahead. Straight ahead. Squealratatatratat."

Flap, Flap, Flap!

"The train, the train, it's coming."

Hendrix flew out of Tom's arms, nudged him with his beak, and smacked his wings just below Tom's armpits. I could have sworn that bird was trying to make Tom fly.

"Squealratatatratat. Let's go. Let's go. Let's go. SQUAWK!"

"Tom," I shouted, "he wants to take you somewhere."

"I can hear that, Indiana," Tom shouted back, over Hendrix's blaring calls.

"What are you waiting for?" I jumped up. "If we don't hurry, I think he'll go bananas."

"I think he already has." Tom's hair was a mess of feathers as he waved his arms to shoo Hendrix. "All right, Hendrix. Lead the way."

"Follow that bird!" I hopped back on my bike. Jamie didn't budge.

"Jamie!" I said.

"Aw, what the heck," Jamie mumbled. "But if my sisters hear that I'm taking orders from a bird, I'm fried."

TWENTY-SIX

Hendrix soared into the warm sky. He flew down Main Street, skimmed the peaked roof of the County Courthouse, then glided through the air across the old Denning Street Bridge. We rode our bikes so fast it felt like we were flying along with him when… POP! Tom's rear tire fizzled flat.

"It's ripped clear through." Tom inspected the tire. "Your dad's gonna be pretty angry, huh?"

"Nope. He loves broken stuff. He'll just invent a new way to repair bike tires, with orange peels or something."

Tom leaned the bike against the concrete barrier along the bridge walkway. "I'll run. Just keep going."

But when we looked up, Hendrix was gone.

"See, I told you," Jamie said. "That bird wasn't trying to tell us anything. He was just agitated from being cooped up by those criminals."

Tom scowled, searching the empty, Hendrix-less sky.

"Or we can go back to Plan…" my voice faded away as I remembered that we didn't have a Plan C, D, or Z.

"Look!" Tom raced to Hendrix who was coasting toward us. He was the picture of serenity until he landed on Tom's shoulder and began cawing, squawking, and flapping all over again.

"Okay, okay." Tom reached up to pat Hendrix. "We're coming. Just slow down a little."

Hendrix took off, doubling back this time to make sure we were behind him. As he turned right on Southeast Avenue, a double tractor trailer squealed around the corner.

"Oh no," Jamie turned a pale shade of gray, "not Southeast Avenue again."

"Stay on the shoulder. We'll be fine." But I wasn't thrilled to get back on the Indy 500 of River Creek again, either.

"Where is he now?" I called to Tom.

"Hendrix, no!" Jamie pointed, as the blur of feathers turned off Southeast Avenue and began gliding above Blue Clay Creek straight toward Big Little Falls.

We followed Hendrix off the road across the grass. Then I kicked off my sneakers, tied them over my handlebars, and started pushing my bike through the muddy water.

"I am not riding my bike down those Falls." Jamie stopped moving.

"And I am? Let's just see how far he's going."

Big Little Falls was hardly the Eighth Wonder of the World, but crashing into rocks, rocks, and more rocks on the bottom wasn't anyone's idea of a cherry snow cone on the Fourth of July.

"Hurry!" Tom called from halfway up the creek.

We trudged in silence, except for the sqeeee-uuuwk as the warm blue clay squished between our toes and under our tires.

All of a sudden I got this heeby-jeeby chills up and down my spine feeling.

"Ah-choooo!"

I whipped my head around.

No one.

"What is it?" asked Jamie.

"What is it?" Was she kidding? I definitely—definitely—had not imagined that sneeze this time.

No way. No how.

Unless...

...what if I'd caught a complex on account of being followed by those no-good, rotten, petnapping Brown-buzz and Messy-red-headed guys, and I was cracking under the pressure? Wouldn't that take the whole Enchilada!

If I'm being followed by a figment of my imagination with allergies, I might just as well become a Secret Agent Super Spy when I grow up and be followed for real by other Secret Agent Sup—

"Crayfish!" warned Tom. "Watch—"

"Owww!" I cried, creaming the crunchy crustacean whose pinchers creamed the sole of my right foot right back. SPLAT! I fell into the wet muck.

"Indy," Jamie called. "Hurry!"

I stood up, muddy and soaked. Flinching with pain, I pushed my bike up, shoved my feet into my sneakers, and followed Hendrix. At least he wasn't headed to the Falls any more. He'd turned again, onto a narrow, dusty, dirt road.

On one side of the road, a beat-up, old sign proclaimed, "Used Tires for Sale, All Sizes." I figured the last time that ramshackle little store had sold a tire it had been to Ernie Evermore's great-great-great-great-great-grandmother for her horse and buggy.

On the other side of the road, clackety railroad tracks bumped along the river up to the old train station.

I walked into the waiting room and nearly crashed into a wooden board poking out sideways from a broken window. Dust bunnies bobbed in the bronze beams of light pouring through the stained glass scenes of Mount Rushmore and the Grand Canyon, scenes that used to fill my head with dreams.

"What is this place?" asked Jamie, standing under the giant, round clock, its hands stuck at 5:18.

"The train station," I answered. I sat on a bench to examine my throbbing foot. "Once when I was little, we took the longest train ride ever to New York City, but then the trains stopped coming through at all. I used to think this was the second most beautiful place in the world."

"What was the first?" Jamie asked, not sounding the least bit interested.

"The lights inside the Lincoln Tunnel… or maybe, the lights on the George Washington Bridge… no, I think—"

"Tom!" Jamie walked to the door.

Tom rushed in, bent down so low, I thought he'd topple over. "They're here!"

"How do you know?" I asked.

"The truck. The black panel truck. It's parked near the old freight loading dock at the back of the station," Tom said.

"You sure it's the same truck?" I winced, as I shoved my foot back into my shoe.

"Sure I'm sure. The Fabulous Flavours gold diamond is peeking through at the bottom, just like in the picture."

"We need to call the police," Jamie said in a "don't even think about crossing me" voice while she did that "don't even think about crossing me thing" with her left eyebrow.

Tom looked at Jamie for a minute. "Yup."

I nearly tumbled off the bench in astonishment.

"Right after we check around." He started back out the door. Jamie planted herself in the doorway, blocking Tom. "No way." She jabbed her index finger in his face. "You said we'd—"

"Look," he cut her off, "the animals are in there—or they were. Why else would Hendrix have brought us here? But I haven't seen 'em yet—"

"Tom's right," I said. "Captain Rodriguez warned us she only gives one free pass and we already got it at the Lodge. If the animals aren't here, she'll never believe us when we really need her to."

"We need the police now!" Jamie insisted. "If the bad guys are in there, they could have... they could have... weapons." Her voice was thin as tissue paper.

"They'd already have used—" I began.

"And they're big. Really, really big. And strong." Jamie bounced from one foot to the other. "Messy-red-headed guy opened the front door—the very HEAVY front door—of the Lodge like it was nothing. Remember? And—"

I did remember, but I decided to make myself have amnesia.

"Shhh, listen," said Tom.

I couldn't hear a thing. There were no sounds at all. No cars, no people. Not even Hendrix, who had disappeared again.

"Jamie, stay here and stand guard," I said. "If we're not back in five minutes, get help."

Jamie shook her head back and forth and twirled her ponytails. "I don't like it."

Tom and I crept along the moss-covered foundation to avoid the mess of broken glass, cigarette butts, and thorny weeds shooting through cracks in the pavement. We hugged the wall of the station and peeked around the building. The black panel truck was parked just beyond the loading dock.

"Can you hear them?" asked Tom.

I closed my eyes to listen.

"Oh. My. God." My heart pounded in my ears. I was sure... pretty sure... I could hear a whimper, and maybe... just maybe... a mew.

A thousand thoughts raced through my head at once, then my breath caught in my throat. I didn't know what I'd do if Maurice wasn't okay... and Princess Penelope... it didn't matter anymore that she would never be mine, but if she was hurt or—

"Indiana, look!" The loading dock's wide wooden doors were opened all the way flat against the wall.

"If we climb up the ramp, we'll have a clear view inside," I said.

"The ramp is metal," Tom whispered. "We'll make too much noise. We have to find another way."

I hopped on my left foot to peer over the edge of a windowsill. "Maybe we can see," I hopped again, "between the boards on the windows."

"Shhh!" Tom motioned. We inched along, our backs to the wall so we could stay on the lookout. The truck was right in front of us. The rusty old latch on its doors was unlocked.

We stared at the truck, then at each other. Tom looked as nervous as I felt. "You think we should go inside?" he asked.

"The truck's probably empty, don't you think?"

"Probably," said Tom.

My stomach churning, I pointed to the loading dock. "The animals sounded like they were over there."

"Yeah." Tom nodded. "Over there, inside the building."

We slipped across the parking lot, cringing as the gravel crunched and crackled beneath our feet.

After a pause, Tom asked, "You want to, or should I?"

But he didn't wait for me to answer. He reached up, heaved the doors open, and up we went, scrambling inside.

Our footsteps clattered on the metal floor, echoing behind us. Then we froze, stunned by the sight that met our eyes.

Cages and crates of animals filled the truck.

And in a back corner, I saw them. Two large cages, a few feet apart. Lily and Esmerelda, looking groggy, but alive.

"We're coming," Tom called, as we began weaving through piled up crates. "Don't worry."

"We'll save you! I prom—"

Twenty-seven

CLANK.

The steel doors slammed shut behind us.

"Help!" I shouted. "Jamie!"

"Open up," Tom shouted. "Let us out of here!"

We tripped our way to the doors, banging and pounding until they shook and clanged.

The engine roared, blasting diesel fumes back at us, and the truck began to move.

"Ugh," Tom protested between his coughs and mine.

It was pitch black. And hot. So, so hot.

I closed my eyes and counted to twenty to get used to the darkness. It was darker than the old coal room in my basement on a cloud-covered night, the creepy coal room that I usually pretended did not exist except that I'd slid down the chute straight into it and Tom just three days ago.

Then it came. The breath-stealing, darkness-pulverizing-every-molecule-of-oxygen feeling, swallowing me up.

"Tom," I said, when I didn't hear him coughing anymore.

"Yeah," he said.

"Did you see Maurice?"

"Not yet. You sound funny."

Funny? I thought. More like suffocating to death. If this getting stuck in deep, dark, oxygenless places was one of those deep, dark secrets of life that just happens to everyone when they turn eleven, I didn't even want to think about twelve.

"Indiana?"

"I can't breathe."

"Yes, you can."

"No… I… can't. No air in here."

"Indiana, listen to me. Close your eyes. It'll help." I could hear him walking toward me.

"I did. It didn't."

"C'mon, keep 'em closed. Pretend it's nighttime and you're asleep in your own bed. Are they closed?"

"Yeah." My voice shook as I answered.

"Breathe in and out, real slowly," Tom said.

I sniffed in and gagged on the stewing aromas of bearlioncougarpuppykitten.

"Uh-oh." My head was spinning as the truck bounced and banged. "I think I'm gonna be sick."

"Put your hand over your nose and breathe through your mouth." Tom's voice was calm and soft. "It stinks in here, but you have to breathe."

"It's not just the smell." My voice was tight and hoarse. "I'm all muddy and gross and… I don't suppose… I mentioned… sometimes… in dark… really, really dark… places… I'm sort of… claustrophobic."

"I had a hunch something was up in the tunnel—besides you thinking I was a bad guy, I mean." Tom leapt off the crate. "But I thought it was the mice."

"Just because a mouse jumped out of your pocket doesn't mean there weren't rats, too." I was a lot more freaked out being trapped in a pitch black, hot, oxygenless truck—by giant, petnapping bad guys, no less—than I was by rats, but the memory of those maybe rats skittering across my shoulders… "Ohhhh," I moaned.

"Just slow breaths. C'mon, Indiana. You're the bravest person I've ever met. You're the one who kept pushing us to follow these guys. You figured out…"

Tom's words sounded all drawn out and distorted. It felt like the time I got sick at Disney World with my cousin Boris in the pink teacup of the Mad Tea Party ride, except a gazillion times worse.

I tried to force my eyes open because I didn't want to barf, but they wouldn't open. I was going to die right here in this truck from stench and suffocation.

There was no time to waste. If I wanted to leave this world with a clean conscience, I needed to tell Tom I was sorry. Sorry for sticking my big, fat foot in my mouth. Sorry for thinking he was in cahoots with the bad guys.

"Tom," I unstuck my eyelids and tried to look directly at him, "if we get out of this alive, I know I don't deserve it, but... I mean... maybe, you know, we could be sort of like... friends."

"Indiana, are you okay? I think your brain isn't getting enough oxygen. C'mon, breathe with me, one, two..."

...seven, eight, nine, ten.... I breathed in slowly, and this time, I felt better. I did it again, and it helped a little more, except sweat was gushing from my pores like Niagara Falls.

I started to laugh hysterically because out of the blue, I remembered that Mom once told me about her Uncle Bernie... or maybe it was Dad's Uncle Bernie....

Anyhow, she told me about someone's Uncle Bernie who wrote that women glow, men perspire, and horses sweat.

"I'm a horse," I thought. I thought I'd just thought it, that is, but I guess somehow or other, that thought popped out of my mouth.

"Horse?" Tom whipped off his baseball cap and furiously fanned like I'd been hit with a dose of instant insanity and only the putrid, hot breeze could save me. "You okay if I try to find Maurice?" he asked when I finally stopped laughing.

"Uh-huh," I said, and he began to make his way through the crates.

Then I spotted them. Dots and dashes of light, slipping under the doors of the truck. I squinted real hard and realized, now that I wasn't caught halfway between suffocation and hyperventilating, that I could see shapes and shadows in the darkness.

"He's here!" Tom called. "Behind Lily and Esmerelda. Maurice the Bear—he's here!"

I followed Tom's voice. "Those blobs—they're Lily and Esmerelda's cages?" I asked.

"Look behind them, where I'm standing," Tom said.

"That big blob?" I stood up and started weaving through the crates to the back of the truck.

"It's Maurice. In his cage."

"Is he...?"

"Breathing. Out cold. But definitely breathing," Tom said.

My body went limp with relief.

"Indiana? Are you okay?" Tom reached for my elbow.

"I'm just fine," I answered, holding my nose and gulping breaths. "So, how are we going to get these critters out of here?"

Tom thought so hard, I could practically feel his brain-waves crashing inside his head.

"My phone!" I pulled it out of my pocket. In the excitement of being trucknapped, I'd forgotten all about it. "It's not working."

"Let me try." Tom grabbed the phone from me.

"Hey!"

"No service. Must be going through a tunnel."

"Don't start with tun... Whoa!" We flew up as the speeding truck hurtled over a bump in the road. "Where are we going? I hope Jamie... Oh no, what if they caught Jamie?"

"Jamie's probably getting help now," Tom said, but his voice sounded awfully wobbly when he said it. He began squeezing past the cages and crates, shining the phone flashlight on each one as he passed, with me right behind. "These cages—"

"Aren't locked," I interrupted, as he handed my phone back. "Are you thinking what I'm thinking?"

"Nobody's ever thinking what you're thinking, Indiana."

"If Hendrix can pry those latches open, so can we. We'll set the animals free. When Brown-buzz and Messy-red-head-ed guys open the doors, they'll bite 'em and scratch 'em. They'll stampede all over 'em."

"I'm not so sure a puppy and kitten stampede is going to make Brown-buzz and Messy-red-headed guys shake in their boots," Tom said.

"It'll be a distraction. Then we can escape, conk 'em from behind, and SOS for help!"

Tom rolled his eyes as he opened a cage, and gently lifted out the German Shepard puppy inside. It flopped in his arms. "This little guy isn't stampeding anyone."

I pushed past crates and cages of purring kittens and snoring puppies to get to the corner with Maurice, Lily, and Esmerelda. I studied Maurice. He didn't look all that alive to me. His big bear body was crammed into his cage with no food. No water.

My chest felt all tight and weak. The longer I looked, the weaker I felt, like whatever had sucked up all of Maurice's energy was sucking up all of mine.

Then all of a sudden,

SSHHEEZUMPHSSSSsssssssssssss

A loud wheeze whooshed out of Maurice's nose as his body heaved way up then thumped back down.

He was breathing, all right. Definitely breathing.

"Maurice?" I called softly. "C'mon fella, wake up." He was still out cold. Lily winked open one amber eye. Esmerelda smiled her goofy two-toothed smile and stretched a tawny paw on the bars.

Tom watched me contemplating Lily and Esmerelda, and I could swear he was doing a Jamie with his eyebrow. He began shaking his head.

"What?" I shrugged.

"You're not thinking of siccing those two big cats on Brown-buzz and Messy-red-headed guys?"

"We just have to climb on top of their cages and set their ferocious animal instincts free. They'll clobber the bad guys. It sure beats us doing the bad guy conking!" I answered.

"No way! There's no telling what they'd do. They're wild animals. WILD. Even lion tamers get eaten up sometimes. More likely they'd jump on top of the cages and gobble us up. You don't see Mr. H. playing with them, do you?"

"I don't see Mr. Humperdink do anything with them." I scowled. "He always makes me leave when they're out of their cages."

I sat on a hot metal crate to think. The three Labradoodle puppies in the cage beneath me looked totally zonked, lying on their backs with their legs flopped across each other's bellies.

"We're cooked," I finally said.

"We can't be cooked. We have to think harder." Tom twisted his left earlobe and plopped down next to me, but from what I could see, his expression looked anything but hopeful.

I squeezed my eyes closed and did the old hands pressed against my temples routine, waiting for the light bulbs to flash in my brain when...

EEEEEEEERRRRRRRRSHHHZZKKK!

The truck jerked to a stop. I toppled off the crate, and my right knee slammed the floor. I'd be lucky if I still had a right knee at all—if we got out of this alive, that is.

Crates flipped on top of cages, slumbering animals snorted and stirred, and a great GROWL rang out from the corner.

Maurice was awake.

The back doors rattled and flew open. I covered my eyes with my hands and peeked between my fingers, as sunlight flooded into the truck.

Brown-buzz guy and Messy-red-headed guy stood at the open doorway, and they were not what you'd call smiling.

TWENTY-EIGHT

"Well, lookee what we have here. The nosy little meddlers."

I was speechless. Tongue-tied. Mute. Not a state of being I was accustomed to. Tom didn't answer, either.

Brown-buzz guy stood just outside the truck, and I couldn't help but wonder what that guy ate. He was the size of a baby elephant when we'd first spotted him at the Loyal Order of the Loping Antelope Lodge. Each time I'd seen him since, he'd grown bigger and bigger, like he'd been pumped full of air to float in the Macy's Thanksgiving Day parade.

"We have some business to do here, and you two meddlers are gonna help. Then it's time for school. Summer school. We're gonna teach you a lesson on how to stay out of our business. A permanent lesson." He snarled, and his mouth curled so far up his cheek it made his eye twitch like a Chihuahua with fleas.

He slammed the doors shut.

Darkness poured in, but I was so shaken up I barely noticed.

Tom walked over to Maurice, stuck his face almost up to the bars, and said, "It's me, Tom. Remember? From Mr. H.'s store?" Then he blasted his voice and sang as booming loud as the entire United States Army band,

"I'm a Yankee Doodle Dandy.
A Yankee Doodle do or die;
A real live nephew of my Uncle Sam's..."

I could hardly believe this was the same Tom Weaver who'd sung that sweet, soothing "Blowin' in the Wind" to Hendrix like he was his own baby bird.

"C'mon, Indiana. Sing!" Tom grabbed my hands and swung me around.

"Hey, slow down," I said, as our hands slipped and we flew apart. "This isn't *Dosey-doe with the Stars*, you know!"

I figured either Tom had cracked under the stress or this was some kind of religious ritual in the face of danger that I sure hadn't learned in Hebrew School. As we sang at the tops of our lungs, Maurice cocked his head. He looked from Tom to me and back again. Then he lifted his left foot and swayed to the right, and lifted his right foot and swayed to the left.

"Tom, listen." Sure enough, all our racket was knocking the slumber right out of the puppies and kittens. "I'm setting them free."

I shined my phone flashlight on a latch and unlocked it, then another, and another, looking for Princess Penelope as I worked. Suddenly, the truck's steel doors clanked open. Brown-buzz guy stood outside the doorway, his tree trunk legs planted on the ground. Messy-red-headed guy stood behind him.

"I'm not done," I cried, as three Dalmatian pups yawned and stretched in their crate.

Just then, a flash of red, blue, and yellow rocketed into the truck squawking, "A thousand times, a thousand times." Hendrix opened the latch on the Dalmatian pups' crate and moved to the next one.

"You are one psychic Scarlet Macaw!" I whispered.

"Get over here!" Brown-buzz guy narrowed his eyes at me. "Time to work, punks," he growled, as I wound through the crates. Tom hung back near Maurice.

"Unload the truck. Small animals in the van. Bear, lion, and cougar—there." He pointed to a green horse trailer. "Happy Acres Horse Farm" was painted in bright yellow on the side.

"More like Happy Acres Glue factory," I muttered.

"Where are you taking them?" Tom motioned to Maurice, Lily, and Esmerelda. His voice was loud, but he couldn't stop it from shaking.

"To a private hunting reserve, not that it's any business of you runts. We almost lost out big time, thanks to you puny little meddlers."

Tom bent down as if to lift a crate. I thought maybe he was crying—and I wouldn't have blamed him one bit, either—but next thing I knew, Maurice was out of his cage, and Tom was singing, even louder than before. I took a deep breath and joined in, coaxing the puppies and kittens out of their crates. Hendrix squawked and flapped, shooing them with his wings. Then he sped out like a shot.

"Hendrix!" I watched him go. "Come back!"

A chocolate brown lab tumbled topsy-turvy out of her crate, and the stampede began. The truck filled with kittens and puppies racing in circles, wrestling, and running straight to Brown-buzz and Messy-red-headed guys.

"You little—" Messy-red-headed guy started toward us. "Eeeow!" he yelped and swatted the air as two Pekinese pups landed on his head.

Tom yelled, "C'mon, Maurice." He sang louder and louder, lifting his knees clear up to his shoulders as he danced.

Maurice danced faster and faster, from side to side, his purple cape swaying in rhythm as he headed all the way down to the edge of the truck.

"Holy Guacamole! I had no idea you could tame Maurice by singing to him and dancing with him!" I mean, I love Maurice with all of my heart, but even I know deep inside my brain that deep inside his brain, he's a wild, unpredictable, dangerous BROWN BEAR.

"You can't tame a bear by singing to it and dancing with it. He already knew how from the carnival."

"I didn't know—" I began.

Tom grabbed my arm. "C'mon," he said under his breath, "on the count of three. Jump! Then run like the wind!"

"One, two..."

We leapt off the truck. Over Brown-buzz guy, who was on his knees trying to catch the escaping puppies and kittens. Over Messy-red-headed guy shooing the Pekinese pups away from his ears. Over the Maltese, who had clamped down on the hem of Messy-red-headed guy's pants and wasn't letting go.

"Hey!" Brown-buzz guy yelled. Juggling three Siamese kittens and one Labradoodle pup, he grabbed my ankle as we vaulted over his head.

"Let me go!" I shouted and kicked—and fell on my right knee. Again. It throbbed and burned, but before I had time to feel sorry for myself, a black and white bundle of energy sprang on Brown-buzz guy's head, clamped on to some bits of buzzed hair that stuck straight up like cactus needles, and chomped.

"EEEEEEEEE," Brown-buzz guy shrieked.

I was free.

"Princess Penelope!" I shouted and held out my arms as she latched onto Brown-buzz guy's nose. "Jump!"

But at that very moment,

EEERRRREEERRRREEERRRREEERRRREEERRRR,

three metallic baby blue state police cars zoomed straight at us from I-70 East.

EEEEEEEERRRRRRRRRRRRRRRRRRRRRRRRRRRR,

the River Creek black-and-white squad car zoomed straight at us from I-70 West.

Clip-clop, Clip-clop, Clip-cloppity-clop. Following Hendrix with all the gumption of the Kentucky Derby third place champion that he used to be, Old Blister galloped in from the Kibble Cut-Off on a collision course with all of them.

"NO!" I shouted, waving frantically.

The River Creek black-and-white swerved to avoid hitting Old Blister, did a three-sixty, and fishtailed into the guardrail with a chalk-scraping-against-the-blackboard screech that stung my spine.

A hair-raising, nerve-splitting, eardrum-busting,

"SQUAAAAAAAAWWWWWK!"

cut through the commotion. Hendrix swooped down in front of the metallic baby blue state police car in the lead before it could hit a single puppy or kitten, bunny or guinea pig, racing, playing, or tumbling on the highway. It slammed its brakes and—

CRUNCH! CRASH! BAM!

—got rear-ended by the second metallic baby blue state police car, which got rear-ended by the third, and all three skidded straight toward Old Blister.

Old Blister galloped faster and faster. Then, like Evil Knievel reincarnated, he jumped up and up and over all three metallic baby blue state police cars, and landed without a scratch.

No one moved. Old Blister, who hadn't heard a thing, neighed with a "What's the big deal?" expression on his face. Jamie and Officer Martin, who'd ridden in on him, were a different story.

Officer Martin's face morphed from purple to red to sick asparagus green. I couldn't see Jamie's face because she'd smushed it against Officer Martin's back, but I'd have recognized that freeze-dried, pancake-flat hair plastered against Jamie's back if I'd been looking down from Neptune.

Autumn Winters. On Old Blister. With Jamie.

"Move, move, move, people!" Captain Rodriguez shouted, rushing out of her squad car. "Block the highway! Get those animals!"

"SQUUUUAAAAAAAAWWWWWK!"

Hendrix zipped across the sky in all his hair-raising, nerve-splitting, eardrum-busting glory. Swoosh—he dipped down into a figure eight over Messy-red-headed guy. He rocketed back to the truck, dive-bombed right into Maurice and whacked his head with one Technicolor wing.

Hendrix was a bird possessed.

Like a low-flying plane, he buzzed Brown-buzz and Messy-red-headed guys. They were making a break for it, puppies, kittens, and guinea pigs dangling from their sleeves and pants. A very angry Princess Penelope dug into Brown-buzz guy's scalp with her back paws, her front paws blocking his eyes so that he had to hold hands with Messy-red-headed guy to keep from falling.

Maurice narrowed his eyes. His mouth turned down. He opened his lips, and all I can say is it's a darn good thing I fell in love with that bear before I saw all those big, pointy, ancient-mummy-yellow teeth.

He reared his head back and beat his chest, and this hungry tummy kind of rumble came straight from his belly. It got louder and louder and ricocheted back and forth, slamming the metal walls of the truck, until the truck couldn't hold that noise inside for another split second, and it exploded outside into the fiercest, most terrifying

"GRRRRRRRRRRRRRROWLLLLLLLLLLLLLLLLLLL!"

I watched awestruck as Maurice unleashed his wild inner bear that had been buried deep inside all along. I was as proud as if he were my own flesh and blood.

Everyone froze.

Even me.

From the corner of my left eye, I saw the nervous twitch of a black and white tail smacking Brown-buzz guy's neck. Except for her tail, even Princess Penelope was statue still.

And then, I swear, someone must have pressed the slow motion button of life. It was like watching a movie at half-speed as puppies, kittens, guinea pigs, and bunnies loosened their grips on Messy-red-headed and Brown-buzz guys. Captain Rodriguez looked like she was walking toward them through JELL-O. Officer Martin looked like he was doing an underwater ballet as he lifted Jamie and Autumn off Old Blister, but it all couldn't have taken more than a second or two.

Maurice bent his knees and pushed off. Off with his arms and legs spread, his big bear body flat as a magic carpet. Off with his purple cape waving, he soared through the air. Maurice the flying bear slammed smack on top of Brown-buzz and Messy-red-headed guys, his purple cape wrapped around them like it belonged to a superhero.

Which it did.

Bone crunched against pavement. Brown-buzz and Messy-red-headed guys cried in pain as Maurice pinned them flat as French crepes and catapulted Princess Penelope up in the air, straight onto Old Blister's back.

Jamie, Tom, and I raced over.

"Why look, you guys," I said loud enough for the bad guys to hear since I was standing even further back than I would have before I saw all those big, pointy, yellow teeth, "Maurice is tugging his left ear. You know what that means."

"Yes, Indiana, I certainly do." Tom shook his head dramatically. "Poor fella must be starving. I'd sure hate to be crushed into a crumpled crepe directly under the belly of an angry, starved, six hundred pound brown bear, wouldn't you?"

We didn't feel any particular need to mention that Maurice, unlike most brown bears, happened to be a blueberry-peppermint crunch eating, lemongrass tea drinking, vegetarian kind of bear.

Twenty-nine

"Mom!" I called, scooting into the squad car.

"Indiana! Thank... Owww," she groaned, as I threw my arms around her.

I pulled my arms away. "What's wrong?"

Captain Rodriguez walked over, shaking her head. "Whiplash, I'm afraid. From the crash."

Mom rubbed her neck as I helped her slide out of the car. "I was going out of my mind with worry when I called Captain Rodriguez."

"Just as I was about to call your folks because I'd picked up the Speed Demon on the Denning Street Bridge," added Captain Rodriguez.

"The Emergency Indy Tracker that Daddy programmed into your phone said you were a 'hungry, hot, scared, brave, queasy, miserable, laughing, furry, blueberry-peppermint-guacamole-craving... Labradoodle?'" Mom squinted at the readout on her phone, "and going ninety-six miles an hour. Then it went crazy and kept bleeping North, North, North. For all I knew, you could have been at the North Pole!"

"I figured we should drive out here to North Highway first," said Captain Rodriguez. "Then Officer Martin radioed that Jamie and Autumn found him after Hendrix found Jamie, but Jamie lost you and Tom when—"

"Aaa-ah-choo!" Autumn sneezed.

"YOU!" I turned to her, but Jamie plunked into the middle of my thoughts before I could say another word.

"Autumn had been following us and was going to tattle on us for trespassing—and a few other things." Jamie looked at Autumn as Autumn looked down at her feet with unusual interest. "But—she saw you and Tom get trucknapped, and then the bad guys smashed our bikes with their truck—"

"Smashed?" I said, "your brand new Black Bomber? The Red Ranger?"

Jamie grimaced and nodded. "So, she gave me a ride on her bike so we could get help ASAP. If it weren't for Autumn, you and Tom might still be trucknapped."

The adults all beamed at Autumn.

I wanted to puke.

Eleven years.

Eleven years of putting up with Autumn's stuck-up, tat-tle-taling, boyfriend-stealing, goody-goody-goody-ness, and now this!

I looked at Autumn. She looked at me. Then she smiled. Not one of her sickly-sweet, fake, "adults might be watch-ing" smiles.

This was a shy, try-not-to-hate-me-smile, the kind that sparkled, just a little, right beside the worry in her eyes.

"Stefano Stefano!" Jamie whispered, and in the nick of time, because I sure as heck didn't know what I was supposed to say, let alone feel, about Autumn at that particular mo-ment.

"Ohhhhhhhhhh..." Jamie bounced on her toes, twirled her curly black ponytails so hard her finger got stuck, and shook her head back and forth in major worry mode.

"What are YOU doing here?" I turned to Stefano Stefano. And not in handcuffs, I was about to add when I stopped cold. "Ohhhhhhhhhhhh..."

"MISTER Stefano heard bits and pieces of a conversation at the ice cream parlor today that made him suspicious of a couple of cool customers, so he called me with a description of them," Captain Rodriguez said, frowning at Jamie for us-ing Stefano Stefano's first name.

"But I didn't see their truck," Stefano Stefano added, "so my description wasn't much help."

I was still frozen at, "Ohhhhhhhhhhhh..."

"You... you'rrrr... yuuu...," Jamie sputtered, pointing at Otto Flavours, the Fourth, a.k.a., Shiny-bald-headed guy, who was standing and smiling next to Stefano Stefano.

"You're under arrest!" I blurted.

"Indiana Bamboo, have you lost your marbles?" Captain Rodriguez said, her horrified expression leaving no doubt about the answer.

"Looks like no one's had a chance to fill in our young sleuths," said a still smiling Otto Flavours, the Fourth.

"Right you are." Captain Rodriguez began slapping him on the back. "Mr. Flavours is a special agent with the United States Fish and Wildlife Service."

"We've been trying to bust up this exotic animal smuggling ring for too long," Otto Flavours, the Fourth, said, trying to keep his balance between back slaps. "It was a lucky break when they targeted Paradise Pets. Mr. Humperdink and I go way back, to his days with the Wonderful Wildlife Rescuers in New York City."

First Autumn. Then Stefano Stefano. Now this—Otto Flavours, the Fourth—a good guy? It sure would've been nice if whoever declared today "Flip the Universe Upside Down Day" had given Jamie, Tom, and me a little heads up, though it was too late now. After all this, I'd have bet Mr. Humperdink's papaya that we were done with surprises for a good long while.

"Officer Martin?" interrupted one of the state troopers from inside the truck, his spindly legs sticking out like potato sticks from his khaki shorts. "How're we going to get that bear off those guys?"

"Leave it to Dr. Debbie. She'll be here any minute."

"Someone call the ambulance," another state trooper commanded.

"Grab those animals!" a third state trooper ordered, pointing to a pack of puppies playing in the cornfield across the highway as Trooper Potato Stick Legs rushed to corral them.

Officer Martin planted himself next to Maurice. While he went on and on to Brown-buzz and Messy-red-headed guys about how they'd rue the day they were born if they so much as lifted a baby toe to escape, Tom snuck up just close enough so Maurice could hear him, and I stuck just close enough to hear Tom.

"This is the last time you'll ever have to dance, buddy, I swear, but let's get you back in that crate," he whispered, and as I watched Tom try to coax Maurice to dance just one more time, I realized I wasn't the only kid in River Creek who was best friends with that bear.

Maurice pretended not to hear Tom. He flattened one furry arm around Brown-buzz guy's shoulders and the other furry arm around Messy-red-headed guy's waist, then tucked his purple cape tighter around both of them.

Brown-buzz guy winced. Messy-red-headed guy looked real mad and real scared at the same time, but I figured they didn't want to do anything to aggravate the six hundred pounds of ancient-mummy-yellow-pointy-toothed, hungry bear on top of them.

Tom edged a little closer to Maurice. "C'mon, bud. The police can take it from here."

"C'mon, Maurice." I swayed from side to side to give him some encouragement.

"The sooner you go back to your crate, the sooner you can get back to Mr. Humperdink," Jamie urged.

"I'm a Yankee Doodle Dandy—" Tom began softly.

"Eeeeeeeeeeeerrrrrrrrrrrruuuuuuuuuggggggggggg"

A long, low moan, a someone revving a sick engine moan, percolated in Maurice's throat. Tom and I jumped back. Messy-red-headed guy's eyes rolled up in their sockets, and he passed out. Brown-buzz guy froze, petrified as the wood in Petrified Forest National Park.

A cloud crossed in front of the sun, the sky turned dark, branches crackled in the sudden wind, and I got a chills-creep-ing-up-and-down-my-arms bad feeling. Out of nowhere, a gang of hot pink, mint green, lemon yellow, and pumpkin orange canaries swarmed just above our heads, like ninja vultures ready to pounce.

Okay. Not exactly like ninja vultures, but they did flutter fitfully around Maurice trying to lift him to safety, except their little wings could barely budge the air, let alone move Maurice.

Then Hendrix, the flying rainbow, cut through the canaries. He swooped down and landed on Maurice's back, pressing his wings against Maurice's shoulder. "UP, UP," he squawked. "UP, UP, UP."

My eyes circled around and landed on wet clumps of fur. Big, wet clumps of fur on Maurice's left thigh. My heart spun around inside my chest.

"Indiana." Tom gripped my arm. "He's bleeding!"

"Officer Martin! He's hurt. Maurice is hurt," Jamie called.

Maurice's arms relaxed their grip around Brown-buzz and Messy-red-headed guys.

"Don't even think about it!" Officer Martin patted the gun on his hip, though it wasn't immediately apparent how they could escape with six hundred pounds of Maurice the Bear still flat on top of them.

Dr. Debbie drove up in her Mini Cooper right behind the ambulance. She uncurled all six feet two inches of herself as she squeezed out of her car, grabbed her black veterinarian bag, and said, "I'm going to give him a tranquilizer so he'll fall asleep. We'll use the ambulance to move him to the Cincinnati Zoo. He's going to need a specialist."

"Hey, what about us?" Brown-buzz guy grumbled.

"What about you?" snapped Officer Martin as Dr. Debbie hurried to Maurice, murmuring soothingly.

"*Eeerrrrruuuggg,*" Maurice moaned.

Dr. Debbie walked out of his sight, and before we knew it, she'd pulled out a monster needle and poked him in the patootie. Maurice's eyes bobbled. His right eye did a one-eighty to the right. His left eye did a one-eighty to the left. His brown fur rippled beneath his purple cape like a wheat field in the wind as a great shudder raced down his spine. Then he went limp.

"Hold him steady—straight as you can," Dr. Debbie commanded. "On the count of three."

Captain Rodriguez, Officer Martin, Ed the paramedic, and all three state troopers grunted as they lifted him into the ambulance.

Messy-red-headed guy groaned and opened his eyes.

"Captain, you'd better get these guys to River Creek Memorial," Dr. Debbie called from the ambulance. "They could use a once-over by a people doc."

"Phew-ooo-itt," Captain Rodriguez whistled. A black limo pulled up, except this was no going to the River Creek Senior Prom, flat screen TV in the back seat, limousine. It was Ernie Evermore driving the Evermore Funeral Home hearse.

"Load 'em up, Ernie," Captain Rodriguez called.

"Not on your life!" Brown-buzz guy protested.

"You gotta be kiddin'!" Messy-red-headed guy groused.

"Your call, fellas." Captain Rodriguez looked at her watch. "I'd guess the ambulance oughta' be back from Cincinnati around midnight, and seeing as how you fellas aren't in any kind of hurry…"

She strolled over to her squad car, popped the trunk, and took out a stadium chair, a Diet Coke, and the *River Creek Gazette*. She put on her turquoise half-moon reading glasses, thumbed through to the crossword, and called out, "Anyone know a seven letter word for folded paper?"

"Newspaper?" someone shouted.

"Origami!" Jamie cried.

"Bingo!" The Captain tipped her hat to Jamie, then stretched her legs. "How about an eleven letter—"

"FINE." Brown-buzz guy snarled.

"Captain!" Dr. Debbie's voice boomed out from the back of the ambulance as Trooper Potato Stick Legs and the others loaded Brown-buzz and Messy-red-headed guys into the hearse. "I need an escort, STAT! This bear's having a baby!"

Captain Rodriguez shouted something into her cell phone. Officer Martin scurried like a pup chasing its tail, but Jamie, Tom, and I were struck dumb on the spot. While we stared at Dr. Debbie like she'd just spoken fluent gobbledygook, Lyle zoomed up in the lime green Lylemobile, tubs of blueberry-peppermint crunch ice cream stacked up beside him like the Leaning Tower of Pisa.

Lyle loaded the ice cream into the ambulance, hopped in next to Dr. Debbie, and off they went, behind one scraped-up River Creek black-and-white in the lead and three bashed-in metallic baby blue state police cars bringing up the rear.

We stood and watched as they grew smaller and smaller, then disappeared inside the invisible place where the red hot sunset met the August cornstalks blowing in the wind, just at the edge of the horizon.

THIRTY

"A penny for your thoughts." Dad kissed my forehead as he tucked me in.

I hadn't said a word, not on the drive home, not while Mom squished me in a rib-cracking hug and wouldn't let go, not even while she threatened to hang me upside down from my toenails if I ever did anything so dangerous again.

I'd wanted to talk. It was just that my thoughts were zinging every which way inside my brain, and I couldn't catch a single one to say it out loud.

When I finally fell asleep, I kept tossing and turning and tumbling down a deep, dark tunnel. Just when I was about to hit the ground, the tunnel morphed into the stinky, oxygenless black panel truck where I could hear the animals whimpering inside.

I was sure I'd die of claustrophobia and heartbreak, when BOOM! I jolted awake, then tossed and turned and tumbled down that deep, dark tunnel all over again, until all of a sudden it was morning, and Mom was standing next to my bed.

"Indy? Are you awake?" She stroked my hair. "Jamie and Tom have been waiting downstairs for ages."

"Ages? But I never sleep past..." My cell phone glowed 10:47.

I leapt out of bed, raced over to the mouse hole in my room, and pulled out P.J.'s food bowl.

Empty.

It wasn't that I wanted that little mouse we saw yesterday to be trapped and starving in the wall of death, but it just had to be P.J. eating that food. I filled up the bowl, left it a little closer to the opening than last time, and went down to the living room where Jamie and Tom were sitting at the top of the Staircase to Nowhere.

"Hey, sleepyhead," Jamie said, as I climbed up to join them.

"Huh?" I asked, still feeling foggy from tunnel-tumbling all night long.

"Isn't it amazing about Maurice? Having a baby, I mean." Jamie smiled.

I shrugged, then noticed that Tom hadn't said a word. I wondered if this time he really was thinking what I was thinking.

I mean, first, Maurice goes and gets clobbered clobbering those crooks, and if that wasn't bad enough to shift my single solitary worry gene into overdrive, it turns out that he's a—

Hold on. Don't get me wrong.

What could be more totally cool than a purple-cape wearing, teeny-tiny bundle of Baby Maurice the Bear? It's just that one minute, I'm drinking lemongrass tea with my other best friend in the whole world, and the next minute, He turns out to be a She. I know. Honest, I do. It's what's inside that counts. But, for cryin' out loud!

He could have told me he's a girl!

"Earth to Indy!" Jamie waved her hand up and down in front of my face. "Is that you or your body-snatching, zombie-alien, coconut-brained double in there?"

"Look!" Tom read the headline to me, then slid the newspaper over. "We're famous!"

GUTSY GUMSHOES NAB 'NAPPERS
Bird Wings Way to Vanished Varmints
Brave Bear Crunches Crooks

River Creek, Thursday morning

With guts and gumption yesterday evening, three
River Creek youths, Indiana Bamboo, Jamie Doo-
little, and Tom Weaver, with heroic assistance from
Maurice the Bear and Hendrix, Mr. Humperdink's
ancient Scarlet Macaw, showed true grit and selfless
bravery as they led police to the animals stolen from
Paradise Pets. Autumn Winters lent this young gum-
shoe gang a hand, as they discovered—

I was getting worked up about Autumn all over again
when my first text message ever popped up on my phone.
Indiana Bamboo—You rock! xo BJ
"Holy Guacamole." My heart flipped faster than an
Olympic gymnast. I guess Bartholomew Jackson had seen
the paper, too. Still looking over my shoulder, Jamie read the
message, her eyebrows drifting in disapproval all the way off
her forehead.
"B.J.," I said to no one in particular.
"Don't even think about it," Jamie warned.
"Go ahead." I gave up and handed her my phone. As my
Grandma Bamboo always said, "Fool me once, shame on
you. Fool me twice, shame on me." I was not about to let
Bartholomew Jackson Alexander McGill take my heart for
another ride on the roller coaster of romance.
"xo B.J.? What a jerk! Though I have to admit, 'B.J.' is
going to work out a lot better for him than Bartholomew
Jackson would have in middle school," Jamie said, as she tex-
ted,
Save it for Autumn.
And that was that.
No more B.J.
No more Popular.
And still no sign that Mom had any plans to get me a
Hanrahan's Department Store Tween Training Bra. We

hadn't even had sixth grade orientation yet, and I was already doomed to dorkdom.

I was about to tell Tom to stop looking so amused by all this, except when I looked over at him, this is what came out of my mouth: "Tah..."

Then I got lost.

In his eyes.

His smoky gray eyes.

It was weird. I mean, I don't even like Tom that way.

"Brussels sprouts, Brussels sprouts, Brussels sprouts," I thought, imagining their yucky, evil grossness to bust any blushing before it began.

Out of nowhere, Jamie blurted, "On the other hand, maybe we should invite Autumn to Fort Bamboo some time. She did help save your life."

"That was an accident. She was spying so she could tattle. As usual." I frowned.

"But she didn't tattle." Jamie started to bounce and twirl her ponytails. "Maybe... we could... you know... be kind of like... friends with her."

Friends. With. Autumn.

Those three words did not belong in the same sentence.

"Think about it," said Jamie. "Have you ever seen her hanging out anywhere with any actual friend besides her frou-frou dogs and her sisters?"

Deep, deep, deep, skin-diving-with-extra-oxygen-tanks-deep down, now that Jamie had mentioned it, I had a funny feeling that she kind of had a point.

"Fine." I sighed.

Fine. Fine. Fine. Autumn Winters, you're on friendship probation, but if the brown-nosing, tattle-taling, boyfriend-kissing, fake-smiling, goody-two-shoes Autumn slithers back, it's over.

Ding-Dong-gong-hello-gong-hello-gong-hello-happy-happy-gong-gong-ha-ha-happpppppppppppppppppppppppp----y.

Mom walked to answer the door, wearing the half-finished crown she was designing for the fall play and the neck collar doohickey for her whiplash.

"Once, just ONCE, couldn't our doorbell stop at 'ding-dong,' like everyone else's?" I pleaded, running down the Staircase to Nowhere.

"How's it supposed to work, Mrs. Bamboo?" asked Tom, as he and Jamie ran down behind me.

"It's supposed to recognize visitors by the shape of their mouths—no two are the same, you know—then announce their names and the mood they're in, but Mr. Bamboo hasn't worked out all the kinks yet." Mom shrugged, as she opened the door.

"Mom, your crown..." My parents. Hopeless!

"Mr. H.!" Tom said.

"Good morning, Horace. I'm so glad to see you out of the hospital and looking more like yourself again."

"Thank you, Jacqueline," Mr. Humperdink said. "I was getting so ornery, they finally gave up and booted me out."

Mom gently placed her hand on Mr. Humperdink's shoulder, ushered him to the dining room table, and had him sitting in front of a plate of chocolate chip banana bread before he knew what hit him.

"This looks as delicious as all those wonderful desserts you've brought over since Gladys..."

As Mr. Humperdink's voice trailed off, Mom chimed in, "You remember how fondly I always spoke of Gladys, my Tai Chi teacher, don't you, Indiana? You know, Horace," Mom added, pouring him a cup of coffee, "Gladys gave me this banana bread recipe for Indiana when she was a little girl and would only eat peanut butter, chocolate ice cream, and green beans."

And forgetting all resolutions to think before I blurt, I blurted, "You never told me Gladys was Gladys Humperdink!"

Out of the corner of my eye, I caught Jamie pointing almost imperceptibly to Mr. Humperdink with her left eyebrow. He was stirring milk into his coffee, but I could have sworn I saw a tear bounce off his banana bread.

This was too weird. Just last week, I never figured Mr. Humperdink for the kind of guy who even had a first name. Now it turns out Mom calls him Horace, he calls her Jacqueline, his wife was that nice lady who I met once at Mom's Tai Chi class, Mom brings him dessert, and to top it off, he just cried into his chocolate chip banana bread at our dining room table. Sometimes, I could swear my mom lives a whole secret life in a parallel universe.

Mr. Humperdink cleared his throat. "Well, I..." He paused.

After a few long moments, Mom swooped in with an uncanny impersonation of General Ulysses S. Grant. "All right, kiddos. Eyes Closed," Mom commanded. "Hurry Up!" She clapped her hands. "Mr. Humperdink doesn't have all day!"

I closed my eyes. The dining room door creaked open and closed, and open and closed again.

"No peeking, Indiana Bamboo!" Mom scolded.

"Geez!" Once in my entire life at my three-year-old birthday party at Stefano Stefano's, I peeked during Pin the Tail on the Donkey, and Mom's never let me live it down.

"Arms out!" commanded General Ulysses S. Mom. "Open your eyes!"

But I was afraid to open my eyes because I couldn't believe I was holding who it felt like I was holding.

"Teacup!" Jamie yelped. "But Mr. Humperdink, my father..."

"...said, 'What's another guinea pig?' But he did have a request. I promised I'd take every one of your new litters."

I peeked, fair and square, with my left eye, and there was Jamie, standing with her mouth open, looking down at Teacup and up at Mr. Humperdink, over and over again.

And there was Princess Penelope, snuggling in my arms.

"Mr. Humperdink convinced Daddy and me that our house is big enough for just one more pet. He said you were cuddling this little cutie every day for weeks before she was stolen."

With Princess Penelope smushed between us, I half threw my arm around Mr. Humperdink for half a hug. "Thank you. Thank you so, so, so much."

I think I embarrassed him, but I made him smile, too.

A real smile. Teeth and everything.

"Indiana, she's your dog," he said. "You name her anything you want, but I happened to overhear you and Jamie talking in the store and thought you might want to consider a spunky name, like Scout, because..."

I have to interrupt to say I never realized before today just how much the adults around here eavesdrop on us kids' conversations. It sure explains a lot, like how Mom and Dad know all sorts of things they're not supposed to. First chance I get, I'm having a serious discussion with Jamie and Tom about this. We have got to be a lot more discreet if we're going to help these adults mind their own business from now on.

"What about Tom?" asked Jamie, though Tom didn't look the least bit upset. His smile was so big it scrunched his smoky gray eyes practically all the way closed.

"Tom's going to help me in the store, officially. In fact, I just gave him his first official work schedule. Isn't that right, Tom?" Mr. Humperdink looked at his watch then added, "Well, I'd better skedaddle to the zoo to check on those animals."

I looked at Mom, who read my mind. She looked at Mr. Humperdink, who looked at Jamie, Tom, and me, and before you could say Maurice the Bear, we were on our way to Cincinnati.

THIRTY-ONE

I wouldn't have thought he had it in him, but Mr. Horace Humperdink made all those Danica Patrick wannabes on Southeast Avenue look like city folks out for a Sunday afternoon drive. In a flash, we'd skidded halfway across the parking lot and were following Mr. Humperdink into the zoo infirmary.

"Shhh!" Mr. Humperdink held his finger to his lips.

We tiptoed single file behind him and sat down on the long wooden bench against the wall.

Maurice was all stretched out on a bear-sized bed in the middle of the room since she'd been badly banged up crunching those crooks. Lyle was feeding her bottle after bottle of melted blueberry-peppermint crunch ice cream. Dr. Debbie stood beside Lyle, and a bunch of Cincinnati specialists huddled next to Dr. Debbie.

We got just about as comfortable as we could get on that hard bench, when one of the Cincinnati specialists pulled the curtain closed. All we could see were big, pointy, brown claws poking out from behind it.

After waiting for what felt like longer than forever—but what was actually seventeen minutes and twenty-three seconds according to the clock on the wall above the water cooler—another Cincinnati specialist yanked the curtain open. Then a third called out, "YOWWWW-EEE! Looks like we've got ourselves a brand spankin' new baby girl!"

Sure enough, there was Lyle with the teeniest, tiniest little thing you've ever seen cradled in the palm of his hand.

The room got real quiet. Dr. Debbie looked at us, one by one. In her calmest, no-animal-would-even-think-of-biting-her voice, she said, "And Maurice is holding up just fine."

Everyone whooped and hollered and whooped some more.

"What's this baby girl's name?" asked a fourth Cincinnati specialist.

We all froze in wonderment

Looking down at the teeny-tiny cub, Lyle answered softly. "Eee-vet-tay."

"Ahh." Dr. Debbie smiled, touching Lyle lightly on his hand.

Then the most unexpected thing happened.

Well, second most, after Maurice having a cub in the first place.

Lyle reached over and rested his other hand, just as lightly, on top of Dr. Debbie's. If Jamie's eyes weren't rounder than basketballs at that very moment, I'd have thought I dreamt up the whole thing.

Maurice was too sore all over to feed Eee-vet-tay herself, so for hours and hours, the Cincinnati specialists tried feeding Eee-vet-tay every imaginable flavor of baby bear formula, but that teeny-tiny bear kept her teeny-tiny mouth closed tight as could be.

My single, solitary worry gene kicked in again, big time, but just when things were starting to look grim and hopeless for Baby Eee-vet-tay, Lyle scooped her back up in one hand, filled an eyedropper full of melted blueberry-peppermint crunch ice cream with the other, and wouldn't you know it? Baby Eee-vet-tay turned out to be a chip off the old Maurice. By the time that eyedropper was empty, she was hooked.

All night long, until the morning sun smiled over the dawn, Dr. Debbie and the Cincinnati specialists tended to Maurice the Bear. And all night long, Lyle fed Baby Eee-vet-tay melted blueberry-peppermint crunch ice cream, drop by drop by drop.

So there we were.

Baby Eee-vet-tay and Mama Maurice, getting stronger by the second, Jamie, with her baby Teacup, Tom with a real job in his favorite place in the world, Mom, who has yet to find a person in River Creek she hasn't helped in one quiet way or another, Dad, who rigged up a blueberry-peppermint crunch crunching baby bottle for baby bear Eee-vet-tay in no time flat, and all of us with a most unexpected new friend, Mr. Humperdink, owner of Paradise Pets, husband of the late Gladys, and a person with a first name after all.

And me, with my heart's desire curled up in my arms.

Princess Penelope Lola Scout Bamboo, henceforth, to be known by her official nickname, which officially, and forevermore... shall be...

Hmmm...

I'll have to get back to you on that.

Indiana Bamboo...

...Henceforth, to be known by my official nickname, which officially, and forevermore, shall be...

Indiana Bamboo, Empress of Adventure...

Indiana Bamboo, Mystery Queen...

Indiana Bamboo, Gutsy Gumshoe...

Hmmm. Looks like I'll have to get back to you on that, too.

The End

ACKNOWLEDGMENTS

I am grateful to so many people for your roles in the creation of this book. My deepest thanks to all of you.

My classmates and professors from the Master of Fine Arts program in creative writing at Manhattanville College, especially Phyllis Shalant, in whose class this book began, Patricia Lee Gauch, Roni Schotter, and Joanna Clapps Herman, a mentor to us all.

Mr. Robert Martin, my fifth and sixth grade teacher, who gave more than was humanly possible.

My readers, Frances Hollowell, Marty Lowe, Alice Norman, Ayla, Ellen Jacoby, and the late William Herman; my writing group and writing friends, Heather Candels, Cathy Allman, Terry Dugan, Barbara Gold, Julie Barker, Bryan Mattimore, Marietta Morelli, Lisa Flores Pierce, and Laurie Stieber; and Alan Bomser, Enid Nemy, Corinne Nemy, Melissa Weiler, Lisa Siebert, Judy Moore, Dagmar and Ephraim, my sisters and brothers-in-law, the Kapell girls, my cousins, Judy Aronin, and Linda, Jon, Nikki, Louis, Estelle, Louise, Donna, and Charlesanna.

My dear friends and family, from childhood and beyond.

Patricia Reilly Giff, your hard work, grace, and kindness are a model for us all.

Jimmy Giff, whom we lost too soon, and all the members of Pat's writing workshop for your friendship, warmth, and enduring support.

The New Voices in Children's Literature: Tassy Walden Awards for selecting *Indiana Bamboo* as your Middle Grade Honor Book at just the right moment.

The Tennessee Mountain Writers and Evelyn Coleman for choosing *Indiana Bamboo* as the winner of the Excalibur Award, and Connie Jordan Green for your exceptional generosity and insightful editorial skills.

Robert Cumming and Beto Cumming at Iris Publishing, for turning my manuscript into this beautiful book, as well as Jill Sanders for creating the beautiful cover illustration.

My wonderful parents, who were my first, tough editors, and my children, for your sweet confidence, fierce encouragement, enthusiastic support, and for catching those errors.

With my love, to David, my toughest, most enthusiastic, most supportive critic of all.

Meira Rosenberg began *Indiana Bamboo* while completing her Master of Fine Arts in Creative Writing at Manhattanville College, where it grew from her memories and imaginings of the small town where she was raised in Indiana. Prior to publication, *Indiana Bamboo* was the winner of the Tennessee Mountain Writers Excalibur Award, a one-time award for a first-time novelist. The novel was also selected as the New Voices in Children's Literature: Tassy Walden Awards Middle Grade Honor Book.

She and her husband have three children who are now young adults, but while growing up, they had almost as many pets as Indiana Bamboo does, from dogs, cats, guinea pigs, hamsters, goldfish, and hermit crabs, to the occasional garter snakes who were banished to a terrarium on the front porch. While she spends most of her time writing and as a writing instructor, she is a lawyer and a former Literary Trustee of the Lorraine Hansberry Properties Trust. When her fourteen-year-old Cockapoo, Oreo, isn't being too mischievous, Meira writes in the kitchen at home in Connecticut. But when Oreo acts up, Meira flees to bookstores, libraries, and coffee shops to continue writing while drinking lots of tea and too much hot chocolate.